The Railway Station Man

JENNIFER JOHNSTON was born in Dublin in 1930. Her father is the dramatist Denis Johnston and her mother, the actress and director Shelah Richards. She was educated in Dublin and Trinity College, Dublin.

Her first novel, *The Captains and the Kings*, which was published in 1972, received an outstanding ovation from the critics, and won the Robert Pitman Award and the *Yorkshire Post* Prize for the best first book of the year. Since then she has written six other novels, three of which have been made into television plays. All her novels are set in Ireland at different periods of this century. *Shadows on our Skin* (1977) was shortlisted for the Booker Prize and *The Old Jest* won the Whitbread Award for the best novel of 1979.

She is married with four children and lives in Londonderry.

Jennifer Johnston

The Railway Station Man

FLAMINGO

Published by Fontana Paperbacks

For my Father
with 54 years
love and admiration

First published in Great Britain 1984
by Hamish Hamilton Ltd

This Flamingo edition first published
in 1986 by Fontana Paperbacks,
8 Grafton Street, London W1X 3LA

Flamingo is an imprint of
Fontana Paperbacks, a division of
the Collins Publishing Group

Made and printed in Great Britain by
William Collins Sons & Co. Ltd, Glasgow

Isolation.

Such a grandiose word.

Insulation.

There was the connection in the dictionary staring me in the eye.

No place alone or apart; to cause to stand alone; separate, detached, or unconnected with other things or persons; to insulate.

The good old OED puts things straight for you.

At this moment, as I write these words, the sky is huge and quite empty, no blemishes, vapour trails, not even the distant flick of a lark's small body.

They used to eat larks' tongues. A great delicacy I've read somewhere in a book. At least we're spared that now. The larks can sing. They have their own peace in the empty sky.

I am insulated from the sound of their song and other realities by the thin panes of glass that form one wall of this studio that I have had built on the hillside just above my cottage. That also sounds grandiose.

To be accurate, and it is in the interests of accuracy that I am struggling with these words instead of colours, textures, light and shade, visual patterns, Damian thought up the idea, and then set to work to build it for me out of three tumbledown sheds. I wanted the sea imprisoned there for me alone. Spring, summer, autumn, winter, to be able to watch it change. Morning and evening, insulated from its reality. Crack, shatter, scatter angry shards and splinters. Ploughing wind driving furrows through glasslike deep grey waves. I can watch. I know that to watch is my isolation. I have no other function.

I dream sometimes of catastrophes.

I remember occasionally in the daylight the shuddering of the houses when the explosion happened. Windows then, taken by surprise, cracked, some even splintered to the ground and for days the smell of smoke lingered in unexpected places.

But now, here, the glass holds.

Over here it is bare. No one visits. Sometimes the cat startles me as he pads across the floor and rubs himself against my leg. He doesn't much like it here though. He will pad for a few minutes, stare with almost unbearable arrogance at the canvases leaning against the wall. If the sun is shining he may sit in its warmth by the window for a while but sooner or later he will retire to the cottage, the comfort of cushions and the purring machines that keep us both warm and clean and fed.

I have an easel now. I bought it for a lot of money after my first exhibition. I thought perhaps I might then feel more like a real artist, no fly-by-night enthusiast. I don't use it very often. I have become accustomed to crouching, hunkered down on the floor, but I suppose as I get older, less flexible, I will be glad of the easel. Its cross-shape gives a certain class to the studio. Damian approves of it.

The cottage is quite high on the hillside. I look west from the windows across rough fields, scattered stones and squat bushes, over the peaks of the dunes to the wide bay. A bare rocky headland to the south and to the north a long spit of sand. There is no sign from here of the village nor of the little harbour from which the fishing boats set out on tranquil summer mornings. How romantic that sounds. That is when I am impelled to stand by the window and watch, when the half dozen boats, Enterprise, Cailín Bán, Girl Josie, Queen of the Sea, Mary Lou and Granuaile slide across the early morning sea. The grey days, the buffeting days, I don't bother to watch out for them, then they look ugly and disturbingly vulnerable. The village is much the same as any other village in this part of the North West, the houses and shops clinging to the sides of a blue-black road. You swing into the village past the new Church, vulgar, triumphant and quite out of place in the almost stark landscape. Three or four shops, a couple of pubs, the licensed betting office, a few cottages, the Hotel and at the far end of the village the new estate, two neat rectangles of houses sprouting aerials from every roof. In the summer Sweeney's shop and Doherty's sell buckets and spades and brightly coloured plastic balls, picture postcards in revolving metal frames and both shops have installed machines for making whipped ice cream. In the hollow between the village and the dunes there is a caravan site, which takes a hundred caravans, permanently placed and discreetly hidden from the road. A great source of prosperity.

If you look with care you can see scattered through the surrounding fields the pattern of the village as it used to be a long time ago. Falling gables and piles of rubble are linked by the vestiges of tracks through the rocks and the whin bushes. A few cottages still stand, re-roofed with slates and with glass porches built to keep out the wind. These are, by and large, the homes of holiday people from Dublin and Belfast, England even. Though you cannot see the sea from the village you can smell the salt on the air and the heavy smell also of the seaweed that is washed up on great patches of the sand in the winter storms. On wild days you can hear the crash of the waves and the grinding of the stones as they drag along the beach.

About two miles out of the village on the side of this same hill is the railway station.

Since the closure of the railway in 1940 the square stone house had been uninhabited, the windows had been broken in the signal box and the wooden steps had rotted as had the gates at the level crossing.

Brambles and scutch had grown up on the permanent way and the platforms were covered with thick grass and weeds. That was until the Englishman bought it about three years ago and he and Damian restored and refurbished it until you would never have known that it had suffered nearly forty years' neglect. It is now derelict again and the weeds are beginning to take over once more. The engine shed by the level crossing was almost demolished when the explosion happened, and part of the gable wall of the house itself was badly damaged. No one has bothered to rebuild, or even shift the rubble, nor I suppose, will they ever. . . . The buildings stand there, and will presumably continue to stand there until they fall down, as a derelict memorial to the deaths of four men. Violent, and to use Roger's own word, 'needless' deaths.

Who is this woman with the cat who lives on the side of a hill and watches the fishing boats on tranquil summer mornings?

I had hoped not to have to explain. Explanations are so tedious for the writer as well as the reader, but having explained the place I feel I should also explain the person; sketch might be a more reasonable word . . . sketch the person.

My name is Helen. Not the name I would have called myself if I had had the choice, but I have learnt to live with it. Two rows of wrinkles circle my wrists. My body is still smooth and pale, spotted quite nicely here and there with brown moles; in spite of that I don't get much joy from catching sight of myself in the glass, just too much flesh and pride.

I was born on a Sunday in 1930. The day of the week always seemed important to me. The child that is born on the Sabbath day, is bonny and blithe and good and gay. I at least had that over most of my friends.

My life was filled with safety.

We heard about the war on the wireless. The names in that distant game stuck in our heads, El Alamein, Monte Cassino, Dunkirk, Leningrad, Arnhem, Hiroshima, Ypres, the Somme, Balaclava, Waterloo, Culloden, Agincourt, Crécy. Nearer to home Drogheda, the Boyne, Wexford, more names. Words in books, newspapers, on the air, once more into the breach dear friends, we shall fight on the beaches, and gentlemen in England now abed have nothing to offer but blood, toil, tears and sweat. Just words. We received small wooden chests of tea from America at regular intervals and delicious pounds of yellow butter from friends in the country and there were no more banana sandwiches at parties. These were realities.

I drew and painted. That's really all I can remember positively about my education. My attitude to the whole process of learning was one of passive resistance. Something inside me didn't want what they were offering me. I didn't make any fuss about it. I didn't break their rules, I merely slept most of the way through more than ten years of education. My lethargy tired them out and in the end they just left me to sit in the back row and draw. My pockets were always full of pencils, finely sharpened leads, that snapped if you pressed too hard on the paper, and stubby rounded soft leads, almost grey on the page and soft enough to smear when you rubbed the lines with a warm finger. The art teacher didn't like me doing that. She liked perspectives, neat lines, colours that matched and stayed inside confining lines. Her greatest aspiration for us seemed to be that we should be able to draw perfectly a cardboard box. 'Just so,' she used to say as her pencil flicked across the paper, straight lines, angles, height and depth. I slept again.

I had great expectations when I finally persuaded my parents to let me study at the College of Art, expectations that revelations might occur, both artistic and spiritual. I needed a revelation of some sort at that moment. Of course no such thing happened. I didn't have the gumption nor the energy to realise that we have to create our own miracles. It was like being back at school. I retreated into my sleep once more. I left the College of Art with a dismal record and a confused dislike of art in any form. I remember quite clearly one summer night about a week after my final term had ended, when I carried all my sketch books, my canvases, the framed pictures that I had hanging on the walls of my room, down to the bottom of the garden, beyond the tennis court, and burnt them. I had to make several journeys through the house, up to my room and down the stairs, across the hall and out the side door. The raked gravel crunched under my feet. The sun was only just visible over the high escallonia hedge that protected us from our neighbours. I neatly stacked the whole damn paraphernalia of my life into a pyramid and lit it with pink-tipped Friendly Matches. As the papers curled down into ashes the smoke curled white up past the top of the hedge and disappeared. The sky shone, a deep blue, as if it had been enamelled by some old Italian master. Three gardens away they were playing tennis. I could hear their voices and the plocking of the ball. I stood by the fire until nothing remained but a pile of shifting ashes, the heart dying. The sun flashed in the western windows as I walked back to the house. My mother was standing in the drawing-room door.

'What were you doing down there?' she asked. 'Your face is all covered with smuts.'

'Burning things.'

'What things? I hope you didn't damage the grass.'

'Just a whole lot of rubbish. Stuff I didn't need any more.'

'Not clothes, I hope. I always like to send clothes to the jumble sale.'

'Not clothes.'

Soon after that I got engaged to Daniel Cuffe.

I remember no rapture. Perhaps, though, that is because of the passing of time, rather than the fact that it didn't exist. The snapshots I have of him are like pictures of some past acquaintance, I am not stirred in any way by seeing him sitting on a beach, or standing by a flower-bed in my parents' garden, his eyes screwed up slightly in the evening sun.

When I first married him he was a teacher of mathematics at Kingstown Grammar School. I see from the snaps that he was quite a nice looking man, with large eyes and a friendly smile. If he were still alive he would have run a bit to fat, in the way that men who have been athletic in their younger days do as their lives become more sedentary. He would probably have lost quite a lot of his hair by now, and he might have had the usual Irish trouble with his teeth. He had a good singing voice.

'Did you not see my lady, go down the garden singing.' I remember that, his *pièce de résistance*. 'Did you not see my lady out in the garden there, rivalling the glittering sunshine with her glory of golden hair.' Somewhat complacently I used to think he was singing about me, my glory of golden hair, but I don't think he had that gallantry in him.

We rented a small flat on the ground floor of a Victorian house down behind Blackrock. From the front windows you looked out across a low wall and the deep railway cutting to the sweep of Dublin bay. It was all urban landscape, but beautiful none the less, always changing with the light and wind, blue, grey, green, and evening, smokey purple and the squat houses lighting up, chains of light rimming the dark sea. At night the sky above the heart of the city glowed and lighthouse signals flashed. The Bailey light, the North wall, the South wall, Dun Laoghaire and through the misty summer nights the fog horns moaned to each other. Distant painful music. There were seldom strongly defined lines, for the most part roofs merged into the sky, walls seemed to grow from the earth; the sea, the sky, the hill of Howth all seemed to be part of each other, shading and shadow, no hard edges. A few days each year were so clear, bright that then you could see the realities of granite, slate and glass, the distant sea walls became three-dimensional, Howth moved closer affirming its solidity. On these days people would look at the sky in amazement, shake their heads and say, 'It's going to rain.'

They were invariably right.

Jack was born during that time. Eight pounds four ounces, all faculties intact. I suppose I was happy and anxious. All young mothers are anxious, most of them are probably happy, niche found, creativity fulfilled, something to love bundled fretfully in their arms.

There was also a little girl. She died soon after birth, a victim of warring blood. I remember quite sharply the pain of watching her die, not because I loved her, there hadn't been time for that, but because of the fact that she had been offered no choice but death. I don't mean to swoop into sentimentality, merely to state the facts, and though the fact of her short existence has no bearing on what happened eighteen months ago, her conception and her death are a part of me.

About ten years later we moved from Dublin to Derry where Dan became the head of the mathematics department in a large grammar school. I remember so little of those years. It's probably just as well or otherwise I might bore you with tedious domestic details. It is a curious reflection on more than twenty years of marriage that all I remember with clarity was the ending of it, and even that memory is electric still in my mind for what most people in the world would consider to be the wrong reasons. It was shortly before Christmas in 1975 and I was alone in the house. I was sitting in front of the fire. I could feel the heat spreading through me. Around me on the floor were the Christmas cards. Daniel always complained that I left them too late for politeness. He was out visiting the parents of one of his sixth-form pupils. I even remember the name of the boy. George Cranston. His father was an Inspector in the RUC. My shoulders had been stiff for days and the warmth was mellowing them. The bell rang. I put the top on my pen and placed it carefully on the floor beside the unwritten envelopes and got up and went and opened the door. A policeman and a policewoman were standing on the step.

It's strange how immune you always feel to violence, devilry. Snow mixed with rain feathered their caps. In the car parked in the driveway behind them some sort of a radio crackled.

'Yes?' I said.

'Mrs Cuffe?' he asked, moving his hands nervously as he spoke.

'Yes.'

'May we come in a minute?'

'Of course. It's a horrible night for standing on door-steps.'

I moved back into the hall and they came in through the door. He took off his cap and banged at it for a moment with his hand. Snow drops sprinkled onto the carpet and melted. The policewoman closed the door and they stood looking at me as if waiting for me to speak first.

'I'm afraid we have some bad news for you. . . .'

'I think,' said the woman, interrupting him, 'we should go into the fire. I think you should sit down.'

'Bad news.' The words didn't have any meaning to me as I spoke them. 'What's bad news? I mean – I think you'd better tell me here. Now.'

'There's been an accident. Your husband's been shot.'

I laughed.

'Cuffe's my name. Helen Cuffe. You must have got the wrong person.'

The policewoman took me by the arm and pushed me into the sitting room. I looked at the piles of envelopes and cards on the floor.

'I was writing Christmas cards. . . .' I gestured towards them.

'Your husband has been shot,' she said.

'Dan?'

'Yes.'

'But how? Why? Dan?'

'He was with Inspector Cranston. Leaving his house. They were. . . .'

'Yes. That's where he was. He went to see George Cranston's father.'

'It seems like they were trying to get the Inspector, but they got. . . .'

'Dan?'

'Your husband has been injured.'

'Is he . . . is he all right?'

'They've taken him to the hospital.'

'Is he all right?'

'We don't know any more than that. That's all we were told.'

8

'Shot.'

I wanted to laugh at the absurdity of it, but I didn't think they would understand.

'Would you like to get your coat?' The policewoman touched my arm. 'It's cold out. We'll take you on over to the hospital.'

I nodded and went towards the hall again.

'Nothing like this has ever happened before. To me . . . to us . . . I feel a bit confused.' I pulled my coat out of the press in the hall. 'Are you sure. . . .?'

'Yes. Quite sure.'

The policeman took the coat from me and held it while I fumbled my arms into the sleeves.

'I don't think anyone would want to shoot Dan.'

The policewoman held my bag out towards me.

'Is your key in this?' she asked. 'You'll need your key.'

I nodded and took the bag from her hand. Forty-seven pounds that bag had cost me, I thought at that traumatic moment. I remembered how I had lied to Dan about the price. I smiled at the thought. They watched me smile. I wondered what I should be doing, saying.

'I suppose you're used to this sort of thing?'

They edged me across the hall.

'It's bad times, Mrs Cuffe,' said the constable opening the door. The snow still whirled in the wind. A rotten, stinking night to be shot.

'Will I turn out the lights?' asked the woman.

'No.' I got into the back of the car. 'I hate the dark. I hate coming into a dark house.' I remembered that I hadn't got a handkerchief and wondered would I need one. Uncheckable tears flow in the cinema. Maybe at any moment that might happen. I had no precedent, nothing to measure up to. It was cold. The flakes shone under the street lights or whirled black in the shadows. Uncouth gaps in the street's façade meant war. Snow whirled in the gaps, lying now on the roads and on the birds sleeping along the railing by the river, heads folded down into their bodies.

The soldiers on the bridge peered into the car and nodded us on.

'Why would anyone shoot Dan?' I asked again as we drove up the hill towards the hospital. I asked it just to break the silence. They didn't reply. Why should they. I knew the answer.

I laughed.

'Maybe it was a dissatisfied pupil.'

They didn't move. Their heads remained stiff, staring out of the windscreen. Didn't smile, gesture. My hands were so cold in their silence. We drew up at the entrance for the ambulances.

No Parking, it said. Ambulances Only. A tall man was standing at the door. I knew the moment I saw his face that Dan was dead.

We took him to Dublin and buried him beside the little girl in Mount Jerome. He had had no choice either, I thought, as I stood by the grave, but then, I told myself, we none of us have that choice. Dan's mother clung to my arm as if she needed my support. My hands were still cold. That is the one thing I know I remember. All the rest is a vague jumble in my mind. Did I feel sorrow? Anger? I hope I felt both of these emotions, but I'm not very sure. My hands were cold. No matter what I did over that two weeks I couldn't warm them. I would wake in the mornings to find these two cold hands clenched across my warm breasts. They felt as if they belonged to someone else. One of my teachers at school had had flat white hands. They looked always as if no blood moved through them. If she touched me I used to find myself shivering with some kind of panic. I was worried by the thought that my hands might become like hers.

I worried about Jack. He seemed curiously unperturbed, rejecting almost contemptuously any comfort that I held out towards him. He stood beside his grandmother at the funeral in his school suit, wearing Dan's black tie. His face was very white, but quite composed. He used to go up to her room in the evenings after dinner and I could hear their voices rumbling on, laughing even at times, being comfortable with each other. The day he went back to school I got on the bus and returned to Derry.

The house was just as I had left it that evening. Two piles of Christmas cards on the floor in front of the dead fire, a fine dust on all the furniture. I threw the cards in the dustbin and cleaned out the fireplace. Somewhere not too far away there was an explosion, the floor trembled under me, the windows rattled. I knew at that moment that what I had been hiding for the last few weeks from myself as well as the people around me was an amazing feeling of relief, liberation. As I cleared out the fireplace I wondered about guilt and decided against it, where was the point or the time for guilt. In the distance the fire-engines raced to a fire, ambulances, army vehicles. Glass cracked and split. The flames burst out through windows flickering into the street.

I was startled by my own happiness. The first thing I did after I bought this cottage was to build a small glass porch onto the front, not so much to protect me from the wind, but so that I could walk past packed shelves of plants each time I used the front door. On summer evenings when I water the geraniums they release a warm sweet smell that clings to my hair and clothes. That is the full extent of my gardening activity. I have never had any aptitude for weeding, grubbing, digging. There is room in the porch for one wicker chair. This has become the property of the cat. He curls and stretches on the two green cushions, digging his claws in and out of the covers, which have become feathery and pock-marked with this treatment.

I sold everything that had been in the house in Derry, apart from my books and, of course, Jack's curious mess. It seemed the right thing to do. A lot of people turned up at the auction and pawed with a certain evil excitement through the labelled contents of the house.

Jack never really moved in here with me. He preferred to take on the role of visitor, making quite short and almost formal visits to see me. Most of his holidays he chose to spend with his grandmother in Dublin. I think he must have recognised, without any words being spoken, my reaction to the death of his father and possibly been deeply hurt by it. I hate to think that I caused him pain. Maybe I merely bored him to the bone. Perhaps if he had been allowed to live we might have grown into some kind of understanding, a closeness.

Who can ever tell?

He could hear her shuffling round the kitchen. Her clogs or rope soles flapping as always at the heels. The murmur of her voice as she talked to the cat. The inscrutable yellow eyes would stare back at her as she spoke. Then they would close, a slow curtain falling. If he shut his eyes and dug himself further under the clothes, he could pretend maybe that this was a dream. I am not in Knappogue, the back of beyond, I am wrapped in my bed in number eleven, Trinity College, Dublin. Warm and comfortable city sounds thrum in my ears. People breathe in the next room, cough, piss in the lavatory down the passage, try to spit hangovers out of their heads with the toothpaste. Sometimes when his eyes were shut he could remember his room in Derry. That was his pride, his safe joy. When he had had to rip the posters and the pictures from the walls, exposing the pale patterns underneath, he had felt such desolation. He had had to empty all the drawers and the shelves, pack into cardboard boxes all his books, records, tapes, papers, throw out old clothes, the past's broken toys. He had felt so vulnerable as he stood there in the dusty, empty room with the pale empty patterns on the walls.

'It'll be all right Jacko,' she had said behind him. 'We'll put the whole thing together again. Everything will be all right.'

'I don't understand why you're leaving here.'

She had laughed and left the room.

She was like that. Inscrutable was a word he had often applied to her.

He could hear her now, coughing. She smokes too much, he thought. She stubs out her cigarettes on plates and saucers. Dead butts and ash beside the crumbs or forlorn in the spilt tea.

Filter tips float eternally in the lavatory. Father had hated that. He would rant and rave a bit and tell her she would be dead before she was fifty. She just used to laugh, bend down over the lavatory and pick the butt out with her pinced fingers.

'I'll see you out,' she had once said.

She had been right.

He heard her going out of the back door.

The bottom of the door scraped on the kitchen tiles. It had been like that ever since she moved in. She never seemed to notice that you have to push the door quite hard to open it, nor the noise it made as it scraped on the floor. It gritted his teeth. He supposed that perhaps he should do something about it, but he always felt that doing odd jobs around the place committed him to the house in a way that he didn't wish to be committed. She had run out of cigarettes. The early morning pattern. He could never understand how it was that smokers allowed this to happen so frequently. She would prowl around the house looking for the hidden cigarette, a half-smoked one in a saucer somewhere, one shoved into the back of a drawer. The car was always the last hope. Sometimes she would find one, a box even, lying on the shelf under the dashboard. If she didn't she would get into the car, just as she was in her dressing gown, hair uncombed, and drive to the village. Of course if he were up and about he would offer to go for her. But he wasn't. He was tucked in his bed listening. There, the car door banged. The engine coughed a little, as she did so often, before it started. Probably a piece of red dressing gown trailed out under the door as she drove away.

She would never have lived like this if father had been still alive. He had been a neat, well ordered man. He believed in tradition, in keeping up appearances. 'Within the structures,' he used to say to her, 'you can be vague, careless, introspective, anything you like, Helen, but you must keep within the structures. Otherwise things fall apart.' He had, of course, been a mathematician.

Father had felt she needed protecting from some destructive demon that he could see inside her. He had tried to explain it to Jack one afternoon as they played golf at Portsalon. Pillars of driving rain interrupted their play, sweeping relentlessly down the lough. Five minutes later it would be over and the grass would sparkle and steam under a hot bright sun.

'Your mother'll be getting wet,' he had said as they stood under a tree near the fourth green. 'I bet she hasn't a coat or a scarf or anything with her.'

His voice had been filled with irritation.

'I told her it was going to rain, but she didn't listen, she just went off down the beach with her hands in her pockets. . . . She doesn't mind getting wet. She never has. She used to say the rain made your hair curl.' I remembered laughing when he had said that. She had the world's straightest hair.

'She gets stiff. After all she isn't twenty any longer. It's silly not to take care of yourself at her age. At any age. She's never had much sense.'

He had looked out through the leaves at the rain. Jack didn't say a word. He had really been talking to himself.

'I sometimes wonder what would have happened to her if she hadn't married me. Drift. She'd have drifted.' He had turned to Jack and spoken almost angrily.

'What's she up to now? Down there. Miles away on the beach. Wet. Soaking wet. What's she up to?'

'She can't be up to very much,' Jack said.

'In her head. Bring a friend, Molly, Jean, someone you can chat to while we play golf. Have a drink in the bar with. Company. Not a bit of it. She just laughed and said she'd be okay on her own.'

'She likes being on her own.'

Dan had been silent for quite a long time. The rain was almost over.

'I have given her so much. I can't damn well work out what else it is that she wants.'

'I don't suppose she wants anything, Dad. I think you're just being a little paranoid.' It had been a new word in his life. He was rather pleased to find an opportunity to use it. Dan laughed.

'Come on. The rain has stopped. Play can be resumed.'

That had been the end of the summer holidays before Jack had gone back to school, before his father had been killed.

'And all is dross that is not Helen.' Christopher Marlow, 1564–1593. Prodigy. Prodigious progidy. Political activist and poet, like Patrick Pearse, d'Annunzio. Heros. Bobby Sands. His heroism was beyond doubt but Jack didn't think that, had he lived, he would have stood up to the scrutiny of the literati.

None of them shut their eyes to keep out reality.

No time to do that if you are to become a prodigy . . . or even a hero.

> Oh thou art fairer than the evening air,
> Clad in the beauty of a thousand stars,
> Brighter art thou than flaming Jupiter. . . .

Helen.

He wondered what they thought when they had called her Helen. Had they seen all that?

'And all is dross that is not Helen.'

Or had it been just another name?

He thought he too would like to die at twenty-nine, prodigiously full of living.

*

She called him for his breakfast after she returned from the village with her purchases, not just cigarettes, but also milk for his Cornflakes and the *Irish Times*. He always washed and dressed before he sat down to eat his breakfast so she had almost finished the paper and her second piece of toast when he arrived into the kitchen.

'The tea's still hot.'

'Mmm. Lousy day.'

He poured some Cornflakes into his bowl and then some milk. He sat silently looking down at it for a while.

'I hate Cornflakes.'

The last time he had been to stay he had eaten Cornflakes several times a day. She said nothing.

'Really hate them.'

He sighed.

'Soggy, tasteless, cardboard. That's what they are, cardboard.'

'Appalled, stunned, sickened, outraged,' she read the words from the paper. He got up and took his plate across the room to the sink. A grey curtain of rain hid the view from the window.

'God what a bloody day. How can you stick it here when it's like this, mother?'

'Five times on one page the word outrage. The whole country is outraged.'

He held the plate of Cornflakes poised over the bowl with holes in it that sat in one corner of the sink.

'What are you doing with your Cornflakes?'

'I'm throwing them away. I hate them.'

'Now I'm outraged. Give them to the cat. Waste not, want not.'

'I don't believe the cat likes them either.'

He scooped the mess into the bowl.

'What's everybody outraged about this time?'

He put the plate in the sink and turned on the tap.

'The usual.'

Water bounced into the plate and sprayed up at him.

'You mean the fight for freedom continues?'

'You're splashing water all over the floor.'

He fiddled with the tap.

'Jack. You're making the most awful mess.'

He turned it off.

'I don't mean any such thing. I mean a man was alive yesterday and now he's dead. That's not fighting for freedom.'

'None of those words mean anything any more. Overworked. Demeaned. Anyway, why get worked up about a man's death? We all die. We're all here one day and gone the next.'

He clicked his fingers.

'It's the snatching, playing God . . . that's what is the outrage. . . .'

'An overworked word. Anyway what do you care? What does anyone care? A handful of people feel sorrow, fear, pain. Something. Otherwise it's just words, news. Manipulated words. Pictures of tight-lipped people on the television screen. Not nearly as affecting as a good play. To get back to Cornflakes. . . .'

'Have some toast.'

'It's cold.'

'I'll make you some more.'

She didn't move, though. He looked at her for a moment and then sat down again.

'Don't bother. I really don't mind cold toast.'

He began buttering.

He always put too much butter on his toast; the thought of heart disease never worries people in their twenties.

'No homemade marmalade?' he asked, taking the lid off the jar.

'No.'

'You always used to make marmalade.'

'I have no time.'

'I'd have thought you'd have had all the time in the world.'

'Have some tea?'

He nodded and pushed his cup across the table . . . she filled his cup and then poured out some more for herself.

'How long are you staying?'

'Just over the weekend. I really should go on Sunday evening, but I may wait till Monday morning. It all depends. . . .'

He took a large bite of toast.

'Depends on what?'

'The weather. If the weather turns good, I may not be able to tear myself away. Have you any plans?'

'I never make plans. I thought of clearing out a lot of the junk in your room. I'm sure you don't want it any longer. There's a jumble sale next week and I thought most of it could go to that.'

He laughed.

'My precious belongings. You have a nerve.'

'You brought everything precious to Dublin. What's in there now isn't even worthy of the name of jumble.'

'I suppose I can't stop you.'

'Not really.'

'If you make a pile . . . several piles . . . I'll. . . .'

'Did you know that the station has been bought?'

'No. Who . . . ?'

'A couple of months ago. Some Englishman. I haven't come across him yet. I thought I might walk over this afternoon and say hello. He's doing the place up. He has one of the Sweeney boys working full time.'

He was buttering another piece of cold toast.

'Damian Sweeney.'

'There are so many Sweeneys. I never know which is which. He won't eat sliced bread according to Mrs Doherty. She has to keep him a pan loaf twice a week when the breadman comes.'

'The Englishman or Damian Sweeney?'

'Don't be silly. Haythorne. Hawthorne. Something like that his name is . . . according to Mrs Doherty. I used to have to go to tea with horrible Haythornes when I was a child. I do hope he's not one of them. He wears a black patch over one eye, Mrs Doherty says. I like the sound of that. Pirates and things. Will you come with me?'

'Where to?'

'To spy on Mr Whatsisname.'

'No. There's a couple of things I have to do. Anyway, it's raining. You don't mean to go plodding off there in the rain do you?'

'Rain'll make my hair curl.'

He smiled somewhat sourly.

She poured herself another cup of tea and got up. She wanted to be on her own.

'I'm going,' she said to him.

'Far?'

'Just out to my shed. I must work. There's so much work I have to do.'

'Why don't you get dressed?'

'I'll get dressed in my own good time.'

She picked up the cigarettes and put them into her pocket.

'You smoke too much.'

She walked to the door and then turned around and looked at him.

'Yup,' she said. 'I do. I enjoy it. I just love puffing all that poison in and out of my lungs. Anything else?'

He shook his head. She left him sitting there staring into space.

*

It was about two miles uphill all the way to the station house. The road could have been better. It was years since the county council men had been along with the loose stones and the tar machine. Not much need really as the road was little used. The occasional farmer with land high on the mountain would pass that way with his sheep, either on the way up to their mountain grazing, or on their way down to the market. Sometimes tourists would come over the shoulder of the hill and stop their cars to look down at the ocean and its burden of small islands. No one, either farmer or tourist, ever gave the station house a second look; in those days, that was. Now it has become a part of the local folklore.

The red brick house had been built in 1903, solid, functional, tailor-made to suit the network of lines that stretched out through the hills and along the coast, opening up for the first time access to the world, for the inhabitants of the tortuous and desolate coastland.

The house stood, squarely, facing out towards the distant sea, behind it the two platforms and the weed–filled track and then the hill, treeless, bleak. The signal box was at the right-hand end of the up platform about fifty yards from the station house. Two or three of the wooden steps had rotted away, and a couple of panes of glass were missing, but the box itself appeared to be in very good order. The white painted words, Knappogue Road, could still be seen faintly beneath the window. The old goods shed was at the far end of the down platform, beside the unused level crossing.

The rain had settled into a misty drizzle, but from time to time a slight breeze stirred, which soon might shift the clouds. The hedges were still filled with wet shining blackberries, and she made a note in her mind to come up with a couple of baskets the next dry day. They never tasted good if you picked them in the rain, their sweetness somehow dissipated with the damp. She and Jack could carry a basket each. She laughed at the thought. He wouldn't do that. He doesn't seem to have that line in his mind leading back to early days. We can't seem to find that comfort between us, she thought. I suppose that is what parents and children should have, some form of comfort, if nothing more. It seems quite hard to achieve. She wondered why he had come down to visit her.

A blackthorn tree marked the end of the hedge. Beyond it the road widened and the station house stood there. The right-hand half of the green door was open and she walked across the road, up one step and into the flagged hallway. The air was musty and damp; over twenty years of dead mice and spiders. Even though it had all been scrubbed out and the walls painted white, the smell remained. The door onto the platform was open, letting a draught run through the hall. She walked over and peered through the window into the ticket office. A cheerful fire was burning in the small fireplace. A gate-legged table and a couple of chairs were piled with books. A duffel coat hung on the door that led out on to the platform. She could hear the sound of someone sawing wood.

'Yes?'

The voice came from behind her. She jumped.

'Can I help you?'

'I didn't hear you coming.'

A tall man with a patch over his left eye was standing in the middle of the hall. His empty left sleeve was tucked neatly into the pocket of his tweed jacket. He was altogether very neat, apart from the fact that he was wearing old tennis shoes, in the front of both of which his toes had made small jagged holes. Or perhaps the mice, she thought. Unlikely. He didn't look the sort of man who would let the mice at his shoes.

His voice was neat too, when he spoke again.

'If you're enquiring about trains. . . .'

She began to laugh.

'It will be a while yet before they will be running.'

She stopped laughing.

'There's still a lot of work to be done before we're operational.'

'I. . . .'

'As you can see.'

His voice was dour, unwelcoming.

'Where did you want to go?'

She didn't know what to say.

'I believe there is a reasonable bus service. You can get without too much trouble to Letterkenny and Donegal town. After that. . . .' He shrugged. 'There are connections.'

She laughed again, because she wasn't sure what else to do. A little nervous laugh.

'Oh no. It wasn't that. I live here. I just came to see . . . to. . . . Someone told me your name was Haythorne. I wondered . . . I used to know Haythornes back in Dublin. Ages ago. I thought perhaps. . . .'

'Hawthorne,' he said, and left it at that.

'Oh.'

After a moment she held out her hand towards him.

'Mr Hawthorne. I'm Helen Cuffe.'

He didn't move.

'I live in the cottage down the road. Just before you get to the village.'

There was silence except for the sound of the saw somewhere out along the platform.

'I just thought I'd come up and see if there was anything you. . . . It must be difficult to manage here. If you'd like a meal . . . or something.'

She felt her face going red.

'I am quite good at managing, thank you.'

Two puckered scars ran from the eye patch down to his chin, pulling his mouth very slightly to one side.

'I seldom go out in company.'

Bugger him, she thought. She turned away from him and began to walk back across the hall. I seldom go out in company either. Bugger him.

'Mrs Cuffe,' he called after her.

Helen stopped but didn't turn around.

'You're wet.'

She nodded.

'Or is it Miss Cuffe?'

'Mrs.'

'Did you walk all the way up here?'

'Yes. For the good of my health. I want to live a long, long time. Goodbye, Mr Hawthorne.'

'Goodbye, Mrs Cuffe.'

When she got out into the rain, she said, 'Bugger him' again, out loud.

Towards evening the rain stopped, as happens so often on the west coast. The clouds lifted and the sky became a delicate washed blue. The distant sea, a darker blue, looked turbulent; white foaming waves licked and curled around the islands. The sun softened by mists moved downwards towards the edge.

Helen sat on the step outside the porch and watched the colours change. The shadows of the trees and hedges below her grew longer and darker. Real excitement always filled her at this moment. All nature's changes are otherwise so imperceptible, this hiding of the sun by the world's edge shocked her by its speed and its awful simplicity each time she watched it happen.

Jack appeared from nowhere and stood in silence beside her.

'What time's dinner?' he asked at last.

'Any time you want it. I hadn't thought about it yet.'

'I thought I'd go down and have a drink in the village.'

'You can have a drink here and save yourself the trip.'

'See some action.'

Helen laughed.

'There hasn't been action in Knappogue since 1798. I doubt if there was any then either.'

'If that's all right with you?'

'Sure. Go ahead. We'll eat about half past nine. Unless the action is too exciting, then you send me a message by carrier pigeon.'

'Right. See you.'

Surprisingly, he bent down and kissed her on the top of her head.

*

Eight high plastic stools along the bar. All empty. Two jugs of warm water and some pickled onions in a jar. The smell of beer, cigarettes and turf dust. The turf dust must be my imagination, he thought, as nowadays no one uses the real thing any longer, neat stacks of clean briquettes beside each fireplace. No dust, no smell, no fleas. Rather tired flames flickered round the structure in the grate and across the room, high on the wall, the TV set flickered in reply.

Do not leave me oh my darling –

Mr Hasson must have seen it before. He stooped, arms outstretched along the bar, over the *Democrat*, his bi-focals slipping slowly down his nose, unable to sustain their normal position owing to the tilt of his head.

– on this our wedding day . . . ay.

Mother will be watching it, a half-smile on her face. As she cooks the dinner she will speak the lines with the actors.

Jack thought how irritated he would be if he were there.

Across the hall Mrs Hasson was supervising the laying up of the tables for breakfast. The white cloths hung in stiff points. Each side plate had its folded napkin. This evening one dahlia stood on each table in a silver cornet-shaped vase.

Mr Hasson looked up from the paper as Jack reached the bar. In the background Mrs Hasson adjusted a silver cornet a fraction of an inch and the men leaned against the pillars of the station, blue morning sky waited, they waited, the long silver tracks waited.

'How's Jack?' asked Mr Hasson, as if they were used to meeting every day. He pushed his glasses back into place again and began to fold up the paper.

'Great, thanks. Everything okay with you?'

'Mustn't complain. The Mammy keeping well? Just down for the weekend? She'll be glad of the company. Give her a lift.'

Want to bet?

Jack thought of her face as he had walked in the door the evening before, quite unexpectedly, like someone being pulled sharply from the safe web of sleep. Pleased, yes, finally pleased, but her mind taking quite some time to reach that pleasure.

'And dear old dirty Dublin? Same as ever?'

'Much the same.'

'Dangerous. Maire McMenamin from Gortahork had her car broken into and all her clothes taken. In broad daylight. Not a stitch or stim left to her. You want to mind yourself up there. Drugs and drink and kids stealing money.' He laughed suddenly and reached for a pint glass. 'That's what they say on the wireless. Guinness?'

Jack nodded.

'They say nowadays it's safer in Belfast. Troubles and all. What would you say to that?' He held the glass carefully angled under the tap.

'It's not as bad as the papers make out.'

He paid no attention.

'I wouldn't go near the place at all now. There was Mrs Hasson only last week wanted up to Dublin to look at the shops. Not at all, I says to her. What can you get in Dublin you can't get just as well in Donegal town? And the price of petrol. And you could lose your life. Have the car smashed up. Lose your life in the night walking down O'Connell Street. That's what I said to her. Wasn't I right?'

'Did she go?'

'Of course she didn't go. Why would she go whenever I told her not to? Save your money I said to her and away on to Lourdes next year with your sister Kathleen. The two parishes is getting together and forming a group.'

He slowly let go of the handle and looked at the glass. 'Wasn't I right?'

'If she wants to go to Lourdes. . . .'

'Of course she wants to go to Lourdes. Hasn't she been on at me for years about it, and the group has always gone at the wrong time. Right in the middle of the tourist season. Caravans full. The hotel full. People in and out for meals at every hour of the night and day. How could she go then? I mean to say. Answer me that?'

'How indeed.'

He pushed the glass over to me.

'There's a new priest here, Father Mulcahy, and I said to him, Listen here, Father Mulcahy, I said to him if that Lourdes trip was at a more expedient time . . . see what I mean? A nod is as good as a wink. Father Collins, not that I'd a word against him, was never very amenable to suggestion. July suited him, so July it had to be. Let's start with this new young fellow the way we mean to go on. Let's have a bit of flexible thinking. That's what I said. Wasn't I right? After all, if you look at it another way, Mrs Hasson works for this parish like no one else. The backbone you might say she is and I wouldn't mind who heard me say it and it's only fair she'd get a chance of a trip like that. Wouldn't you say so? And her the backbone.'

'Definitely.'

He looked pleased.

'That'll be one pound and five pence. God be with the days Guinness was one and six a pint. I don't know how the young fellows can afford to drink at all these days. The politicians have the country ruined. Ruined into dire straits. Wouldn't you say? One and six. And that was real money. Silver was silver. They stole the money out of our pockets when they changed all that. Daylight robbery.'

Jack handed him the money.

'I took the pledge at the age of sixteen and never broke it. Forty-seven years. Think of that now. Think of all the money would have flowed out of my trouser pocket in all those years. Mrs Hasson will take a drop from time to time. A wedding or such like. A glass of port or a nice brown sherry, but never a drop has passed my lips. My old mother, God rest her, always used to say. . . . Good evening sir.'

Jack snatched his glass from the bar and fled to a small table by the fireplace. A tall man in a tweed suit walked across the room. He wore a black patch over one eye and his left sleeve was empty. Mr Hasson folded away the paper.

'Good evening, Mr Hasson. A better evening.'

His voice was English. An Oxford and Cambridge sort of a voice, quite low, quite pleasant.

'Just what we were saying, sir, before you walked in the door. A Scotch, sir? What a fine country we'd have, sir, if only we had the weather. Paradise I'd say it'd be.'

'Full of happy tourists?'

'That'd be the way, sir.'

'Hmmm.'

He turned away and looked at the screen.

A lonely man walked down the street. People waited behind the windows. Watched.

'Ah, yes . . . ' he said, nothing more.

Mr Hasson poured a large Scotch in silence. When he had finished he put it on the bar and pushed the water jug along beside it.

'Good man. That's the ticket. No water thanks. I like it just as it is. I hate your dream of tourists. So here's to the rain.'

He took a drink, then he walked across the room to the fireplace. He stood looking down at Jack for a moment.

'Mind if I join you?'

'No . . . I . . . of course not.' Jack gestured at the chair across the table.

'Thanks.'

He put his drink down on the table and pulled the chair round so that it was no longer facing towards the television set. He sat down.

'Seen the damn film seven times,' he said. 'But maybe I'm disturbing you?'

'No. I've seen it twice.'

'I've always thought it was a bit over-rated. Mind you,' he laughed abruptly, 'I've never seen it with two eyes. Maybe it's better with two eyes.'

Jack shut one eye and looked at the screen for a moment.

'It seems much the same.'

The man held his hand out across the table towards Jack.

'Roger Hawthorne.'

Jack took it. His fingers were cold. He wore a gold signet ring on his little finger.

'Jack Cuffe.'

He withdrew his hand quite abruptly and they sat in silence.

'I suddenly felt the need for company,' he said at last. 'A sickness from which I seldom suffer. I am not the most. . . . Just occasionally . . . a great urge to see a face, hear a voice. I haven't seen your face before around here, have I?' He paused and looked at Jack carefully. 'Perhaps I was rude to your mother earlier in the day. Your mother? Your aunt, perhaps.'

'My mother. She said she might go and visit you. I don't suppose she minded. She's sometimes quite rude to people herself.'

'Gregarious was the word I was looking for. It's strange isn't it the way words elude you from time to time. Play hide and seek with you. I am not the most gregarious of people. Your mother walked through the rain.'

'She doesn't mind the rain. She hates driving.'

'I walked down here myself this evening. It's quick coming down. Healthy. I sometimes regret my foolishness when I'm walking home. I have a specially converted car.'

'Oh.'

The gun battle flickered behind his head. Beyond the door Mrs Hasson was calling to someone in the kitchen. Mr Hasson unfolded the paper again and spread it once more on the bar.

This is intolerable, Jack thought. I will have to go.

'Are you interested in the railway signal system?'

'I . . . not really. I don't know very much about it.'

'What a pity. You could have come up and looked at my box. It's really in amazing working order after all these years.'

Mr Hasson looked up from the paper and winked at Jack over the man's head.

'It's criminal the way they've neglected boxes all over the country. England too. If they'd even kept up minimum running repairs it would have saved them so much money in the long run.'

'I can't see. . . .'

'They'll have to open the branch lines again, you know. The day is coming very soon. I just thought you might be interested.'

'Well. . . .'

'I have been very lucky really. The box itself has taken a bit of a beating . . . some steps gone, a bit of rot. Nothing though that I can't cope with. I have this chap giving me a hand.' He laughed. 'No. More, much more than that. We'll have it in first-class order very soon now. Everything in working order. Damian Sweeney. A really very interesting young man. In other times he would have made a most superior cabinet maker. Marvellous hands . . . imagination. A craftsman. It's good to meet a real craftsman.'

His eye looked sadly at the smouldering briquettes.

'So few people,' he said. 'So few people.'

His eye moved from the fire to Jack's face. He protected himself by taking a gulp of beer.

'Perhaps you know him?'

'Not really. I came across him when my mother moved here first. We had a bit of a barny.'

'I take it that means a fight? Fisticuffs.'

Jack nodded.

'He called me a West British bastard.'

'Ah, yes. Yes.'

'So a bit of blood was drawn. Nothing serious. I don't really live here. I just appear for a few days now and then.'

'He holds a piece of wood in his hand as if it were alive. We don't talk much. We just work together. It is a very good feeling.'

Jack wondered what Damian was up to, working for such an oddball.

'Perhaps you would allow me to buy you another drink?'

'I. . . .'

'Seeing as how I have imposed my company upon you.'

'That's very kind of you.'

He nodded and called over his shoulder to Mr Hasson.

'Could we have another drink for this young gentleman here please, Mr Hasson?'

'Right away, sir.'

'You've bought the railway house?' Jack asked rather foolishly.

'Throw a couple of bits of turf on the fire for me, would you, Jack, there's a good lad.'

He got up and took some turf from the basket and placed them carefully on the fire.

'It has taken me several years to find the place. This possibility of perfection.'

Jack wiped his fingers on the leg of his jeans and sat down again. The man didn't seem to have noticed his movements at all.

'I had a splendid station in Northumberland, but they wouldn't let me stay there.'

'Why not? Who. . . ?'

He looked at Jack and smiled.

'They didn't think it was seemly.'

What an odd word, Jack thought. One half of his face was seemly, fleshed out, quite precise in its good looks, the other half a travesty of seemliness.

Mr Hasson came out from behind the bar with my drink in his hand and plodded across the room. He put the full glass down on the table and picked up the empty one.

'Jack here's at Trinity,' he said. 'Trinity College Dublin. A famous seat of learning. Maybe you've heard tell of it?' He spoke slowly and with great precision as if he were speaking to a child, or a foreigner. Jack felt himself blushing.

'A very famous seat of learning indeed,' agreed Mr Hawthorne. When he smiled the scar down his cheek puckered and the skin over his jaw tightened with the strain. 'I had thoughts of going there myself once. My mother was Irish. It seemed appropriate at the time, but my education, that is my formal education ended somewhat abruptly at the age of eighteen. I was misguidedly led to believe that my country needed me.'

Mr Hasson winked at Jack again.

Grace Kelly was standing there crying.

'We are very foolish when we are eighteen.' Mr Hawthorne looked at Jack. 'You, I take it, have passed that foolish age.'

'He's a very clever fellow,' repeated Mr Hasson, moving away from the table. He tapped his head with his finger in case Jack hadn't got the message.

I must face a man who hates me – the music crescendoed –

'I'm in my third year.' – or lie a coward, a craven coward –

'What . . . if I may be inquisitive?'

– or lie a coward in my grave.

'Politics and economics.'

'Didn't I say he was clever?' Mr Hasson stepped in behind

the bar and lifted his eyes to the screen. The serious shooting was about to begin.

'Little did she think in them days she'd end up a princess.'

The man, Roger Hawthorne, smiled again.

'Is that interesting?'

'I thought it was going to be . . . but . . . I'm not quite sure what I'm doing there.'

'It's breathing space.'

'Or a waste of time.'

'I presume you're quite intelligent.'

Jack laughed. 'Quite.'

'Then the time probably isn't being wasted. I have spent almost half my life in hospital. One sort of hospital or another. From the age of nineteen. That is wasting time. They sew you together, mind as well as body and try to make you acceptable to society. Be thoughtful of the feelings of others. Don't show people your scars. Be a good brave boy.'

Oh hell, Jack thought.

'It's all right. You don't have to worry. I'm not going to show you my scars. Any of them.'

He took a long drink. 'For how long are you here?'

'Just a couple of days. I come down from time to time to see my mother. She's alone.'

'Oh.'

'My father's dead.'

'Oh.'

'He was killed in the North. Derry. We used to live there. 1975.' He always felt that it was best to get that over.

'Oh, I see,' was all he said.

After quite a long time he spoke again. 'You must come up and look at my box.'

'Box? . . . oh, yes.'

Damian.

'Yes. I'd like to do that.'

'Come tomorrow. He's working seven days a week at the moment. He should have finished the steps tomorrow. Damian that is. If you feel like it come tomorrow.'

He stood up abruptly. 'I have imposed myself upon you for too long. Forgive me.'

'Please don't . . . I . . . .' He indicated my glass of beer.

The man moved his mouth in a slight grimace. He nodded

towards Jack and picked up his glass. He turned away and walked across the room to the far end of the bar. Jack noticed as he walked that his head was pulled slightly to the left as if the left-hand side of his body was slightly shorter than the right.

It was all music now and a happy ending.

What should I do if you leave me?

He pulled himself up on one of the black plastic stools and indicated silently to Mr Hasson that he would like another drink.

Do not forsake me oh my darling on this our wedding day. Do not forsake me oh my darling. . . .

Jack swallowed down his beer as quickly as he could.

'Goodnight,' he said as he left the bar.

'Night, Jack,' said Mr Hasson cheerfully. He gave a final wink as he spoke. Roger Hawthorne didn't say a word.

*

She was sitting apparently staring at the reflection of herself in the dark window of the sitting room. The reflection of the warm room was like a blind keeping out the darkness and yet at the same time meshed with the darkness.

'You missed *High Noon*,' she said, standing up as Jack came in.

'No. I got *High Noon*. I'm thinking of starting a campaign for the suppression of *High Noon* in public places . . . and *Casablanca*, come to think of it.'

'I thought you were well reared.'

'*Stagecoach* and *Maltese Falcon*.'

'You're quite disgusting.'

'And Cornflakes.'

She went into the kitchen.

'Such foolishness . . .' she said as she passed him. 'Come and eat. No Cornflakes tonight.'

He followed her in and sat down at the table.

'I met your friend.'

'Who?' she asked, taking things out of the oven. 'Open that wine, like an angel. I have no friends.'

'The station man. Mr Hawthorne.'

'Oh, him. Hardly a friend.'

'Damn, the cork's broken.'

'Well, don't mess about with it, push it in. Push it in, Jack. Where did you come across him?'

'In the hotel. He also was rather bored by *High Noon*. He sort of apologised for being rude to you.'

'Fancy that.'

She put a plate of food in front of him. She had always had the idea that a good mother's function was to feed her young.

'I think he's probably a bit mad. He wants me to go up and look at his signal box. Mother, I'll never wade through all that.'

'Try,' was all she said.

She took the wine bottle out of his hand and pushed her fingers down the neck moving the remains of the cork to one side so that she could splash out a first glass without too much trouble.

'Your father always mucked up the corks in wine bottles too.'

'Cheap wine has cheap corks.'

'Rubbish. He just had a somewhat insular attitude towards wine, so he didn't take care. All you need is a little care. Put the corkscrew in straight for starters. Look at that.'

She picked up the corkscrew and waved it under his nose.

'Okay. Okay. I get the message.'

She sat down and looked at the food in front of her. She had given herself almost as much as she had given Jack. No wonder she was getting fat, he thought. Fat and crabbed. She grinned at him suddenly.

'Tell me more about your man above. The Long John Silver type.'

'I don't know much more. He just seems to have this thing . . . fantasy . . . madness . . . I don't know which, about signal boxes. He said he had a station in England somewhere before he came here. A bloody Capitalist with more money than sense, if you ask me.'

She usually went a little red in the face when he said that sort of thing. Blushed for what she considered to be his crassness. He always resented that. She didn't necessarily say anything, just blushed. They both ate in silence for a moment.

'He said Damian Sweeney is an artist,' Jack said at last.

'Is he the one you had the fight with?'

'Yes.'

She laughed.

'I remember that. Blood is so bright. I don't remember why or anything like that, just the bright blood on your shirt when you came to the door. Someone told me he was mixed up in something.'

She pulled a cigarette out of a box on the table and tapped the end of it with her thumb, then for some reason or other she put it back in the box again.

'Oh,' was all he said.

'He's a Socialist or something.'

'Fairly harmless, mother. I'm a Socialist.'

'There are Socialists and Socialists.'

'A profound remark.'

She looked across the table at him and smiled slightly.

'I don't pretend to understand.'

'Everyone should try. It's a duty to try.'

She shook her head.

'I feel no sense of duty.'

He wondered what she did feel, but of course he didn't ask her. There had always been some barrier between them that inhibited that sort of question.

'A member of some violent and utterly illegal organisation,' she said after a long time. 'I think that's what I was told.'

'You mean a freedom fighter?'

'We have freedom.'

This time she took the cigarette out of the box and put it in her mouth.

'You don't know what you're talking about.'

'Probably not, but then I don't think you do either. Truth gets lost so easily.'

'What on earth do you know about the truth of things? The actuality. You sit on the side of this hill and stare at the sea. Your house is warm, you have enough to eat, nobody bothers you. What have you ever known about anything – ' She just smoked her cigarette.

'It's one of the great enemies we have to fight against. Bourgeois complacency.'

'There's not much point in yelling slogans at me.'

'I'm not yelling slogans.'

'Maybe not but you're getting all worked up to it.'

'You have to yell at people who don't . . . won't listen.'

'I don't have to listen if I don't want to. That's one of the things freedom is about. Anyway, when you've something new to say . . . oh God, when anyone has something new to say I will listen . . . even here on the side of the hill. One of the few privileges of growing older is that you can choose.'

Jack laughed at that luxurious notion.

She squinted her eyes together and looked at him through the cloud of her own smoke.

'You should never hold anyone in contempt,' she said quietly. 'No one ever in contempt. You can hate them . . . whatever . . . hate me if you want, but the other, no.' She moved the hand with the cigarette suddenly in an arc through the air and ash fell onto the table.

'I don't hold you in contempt,' he said rather indignantly.

She stubbed the cigarette out and continued with her food in silence.

Why do we find it so hard to speak?

He didn't want to speak to her. That is the gut of it. He didn't want her to know his secrets. He had learnt that from her. She had protected her secrets from them, Dan and himself. Quite a ruthless protector of secrets she had always been.

'He must have been very handsome when he was whole,' she said at last. 'I wonder what happened to him?'

'Who?' He was lost.

'That railway station man.'

'The war, I think.'

'Ah, yes. The war.'

'Have some more?'

'I couldn't eat another thing.'

'An orange? Have an orange.'

'I hate oranges, mother. I've always hated oranges. You ought to know that by now.'

'Yes. I always forget. I can't ever understand how anyone could hate oranges. Perhaps one day a miracle will happen. Pow, bam, you'll eat an orange.'

'Why do you never come up and visit Gran?'

'I don't visit anyone.'

'She'd like you to.'

'Mmmm.'

'Just a couple of days from time to time.'

'We were never the best of friends.'

'That's not what she says. She's terribly fond of you. She misses seeing you.'

'Your grandmother has lots of people to see. She has the three girls fussing round her like slaves . . . as well as all her friends. Not having me around doesn't make any hole in her life.'

'Dad. . . .'

'Listen Jack . . . I was a dutiful wife, a dutiful daughter in law . . . that's all over now.'

She poured herself another glass of wine. 'There's so little time left.'

'For her.'

'For me. I don't want to be sucked back into anything again. I don't want to be mauled about.'

'You're nuts.'

'Yup.'

'What'll I say to her?'

'Nothing. Don't carry messages. Don't you remember the Greek tragedies . . . it was always the messengers had their eyes gouged, their tongues cut out. Believe you me, if your grandmother wants to see me, she'll let me know herself.'

She stretched her hand out across the table towards him.

'It's okay, pet. You and she get on. That's fine. As it should be. Your father never quite shook her off his back . . . he never wanted to. She treated him as if he were some sort of superior being. He found that irresistible. I see no reason why you shouldn't find it irresistible also, only I don't have to be involved this time.'

He stood up.

'I'm going to bed.'

She nodded.

'I'll just have another cigarette and then I'll go.'

'How many do you smoke a day?'

'Too many.'

He left her to it.

*

It must have been the day after that that she found the old wind-up gramophone. Jack had gone out some time in the middle of the morning. Rain had been pecking at the glass roof of the shed and she heard him crash the gears of the car as he turned out of the gate and drove up the road away from the village. Her head was filled with jaded thoughts. There are those times when lethargy seems to embrace you so closely you feel the weight of it physically with each step, each gesture of the hand. Even to pick up a cigarette becomes a major operation. Nothing fresh pushes its way into your mind. Such days, weeks, sometimes even months, she found it hard to move out of bed in the morning. A day without hope is better spent in bed. She was convalescing after such a bout and had just started to look somewhat gingerly at her work. The excuse to leave the small shed for an hour or two of burrowing through Jack's rubbish was too good to miss.

The side of the room in which he lived was neat. His bed was carefully made, the notebooks and papers on his desk in ordered piles. A small portable typewriter was covered with a blue cloth. That desire for visible order he had inherited from his father. She had never cared for neatness. Along the wall at the other end of the room were stacked two trunks and several teachests all protected from the dust by a couple of pairs of old curtains. She opened the first trunk. Two old blazers, some distorted shoes, a tennis racquet, a Maxply, grip unwinding: Jack had played quite well, probably still did, a good strong forehand drive and an accurate service, also inherited from his father. Posters, rolled neatly and pushed down the back of the trunk. The usual Che Guevara, Mick Jagger, Monroe, Chaplin and a copy of the Proclamation. A box of snapshots that he had taken himself with the Kodak Instamatic that she had given him for his tenth birthday. They showed no great signs of originality. A few books, none of them interesting, Alistair Maclean, Agatha Christie, the rest had gone to Dublin; a few more books that had been hers when she was a child, *Alice*, the *Crimson Fairy* book, *Just So Stories*, her name carefully written on the first page in large unjoined letters, *Treasure Island*, *The Black Arrow*, Kingsley's *The Heroes*. She gathered them into a pile and brought them out and put them on the kitchen table. The pages of the *Crimson Fairy* book had golden edges. The cat had been eating the butter and crouched beside the empty dish daring her to hit him. She took away the smeared dish and washed it and lit the gas under the remains of Jack's breakfast coffee.

'Bloody awful cat,' she said. 'If you dare get sick in the house

I will hit you.' He flicked her words away from around his ears and went asleep.

It's strange how one person's words sound so loud in an empty room. They resound, unlike a conversation which seems to become absorbed by the surrounding objects.

She liked from time to time to confront herself with the sound of her own voice. Oral images can be as exciting, as mind-stirring as visual ones. The spoken words echo, flicker with their own resonances in your head.

The coffee was disgusting. She left it after two sips and went back to Jack's room.

The gramophone was in the second trunk, underneath a carefully padded and packed pile of old shellac records. It was awkward to lift and quite heavy. She got it onto the desk and gave the lid a rub with the sleeve of her jersey. A large mahogany box with little shutters in the front. Her father had given it to her for her birthday one year . . . it must have been round about the end of the war. She turned the knob at the side and the shutters opened. She lifted the lid. The handle was slotted into its place and there was even a box of needles. She took the handle out and fitted it into the hole in the side and turned it. It creaked slightly as it turned. It had always done that right from the first day she got it. She recognised the sound, and the slight resistance as she pushed the handle round. Having wound it up fully, she carefully began to unpack the records.

*

At the far end of the hedge a gate led through onto the platform just beside the signal box. Someone was whistling; no formal tune, just a high rather breathless sound. Jack walked towards the gate. The base of the signal box was red brick, about eight feet high. A flight of wooden steps went up from the end of the platform to the glass door of the box itself. Damian was crouched sandpapering the newel post at the bottom of the hand rail. One hand moved round and round scouring, the other followed feeling the wood for lumps and harshnesses. A fine dust scattered in the slight breeze. He whistled. He wore a black knitted hat pulled well down over his ears. Jack stood just outside the gate and watched for a few moments. Damian scoured and whistled. The whistling might almost have been a scouring of his head.

'Damian.' He pushed the gate open and went onto the platform. Tufts of grass and groundsel grew up through cracks in the surface. Where once the tracks had been was now a mess of brambles and scrub.

Damian stopped work and after a moment stopped whistling as he looked up at Jack. One hand marginally moved the position of the black hat.

'Ah yes,' he said. 'We don't see much of you about, these days.'

'Work. Exams. You know the way it is.'

'Oh, aye.'

He turned away. He ran his left hand over the top of the newel post and then down the length of it, feeling the smoothness, then he began his scouring once more.

'Ever heard tell of Manus Dempsey?' Jack asked at last.

'Uh huh.'

His hand never stopped moving round and round. Tiny particles of dust flew from under his fingers and floated to the ground.

Jack walked right over to him.

'Manus said he thought we ought to get acquainted.'

The hand slowed down. Damian looked up and smiled slightly.

'Haven't we been acquainted for years. Did you not tell Manus Dempsey that?' He laughed.

'Did you not tell Manus Dempsey I gave you a bloody nose?'

'It didn't seem very relevant.'

'Anyway I don't care very much for the same fella. A bit big for his boots. A Dublin swank. Maybe you're a bit of a Dublin swank yourself?'

'No. I don't think so.'

'Good. Otherwise I might have to give you another bloody nose.'

'You haven't changed much.'

'Nobody changes much. From the cradle to the grave. You learn to walk and talk and fight your corner. That's about it.'

'He says you're a real craftsman.'

Damian started to rub vigorously once more.

'Manus Dempsey wouldn't know a craftsman from an undertaker.'

Jack laughed. 'Not Manus. Him. The Englishman, Hawthorne or whatever his name is.'

Damian looked pleased. 'Did he say that?'

'Yup. A real craftsman.'

Damian put the sandpaper down on one of the steps and ran his hands down the full length of the post. Gently he did it, as if he were touching a human being. 'Feel that,' he said.

Jack moved over beside him and touched the wood. It was smooth all right.

'Like a baby's bottom,' said Damian. 'A few coats of paint now and they'll be first-class.'

A bit of wood was always just a bit of wood to Jack, but the whole job certainly looked most professional. 'It's a pity you have to paint it. It looks great like that.'

Damian fished a cigarette packet out of the pocket of his overall.

'First-class,' Jack said encouragingly.

Damian held the packet out towards him without a word.

'No thanks. I don't.'

'The first today.' He took a cigarette out of the packet and stuck it in his mouth. 'I don't know why I do it really. I'm not wild about them. I could give it up tomorrow.'

'That's what everybody says.'

'I mean it. That's the difference between me and everybody else. I mean what I say.'

'Everybody says that too.'

Damian took the cigarette out of his mouth and threw it away into the brambles on the railway line. Then he took the packet out of his pocket and threw it after the cigarette. He took a box of matches out of the same pocket and looked at it for a moment. He put it back into his pocket again. 'I'll keep that,' he said. 'In case I want to set fire to you.'

He sat down on the bottom step and took off his hat. His hair was quite long. Soft red brown curls, rather like a girl. He wiped his face with his hat and then put it down on the step beside him.

'What do you want?'

'I only came to say hello.'

'Manus sent you all the way from Dublin to say hello?'

'Something like that.'

He stared past Jack over the hedge, over the sloping fields towards the sea. 'Want to see the box?' he asked after a long silence. He jerked his head as he spoke, upwards towards the door.

'Okay.'

'I'll call him.'

'Couldn't you. . . ?'

'It's his box.'

'What on earth are you doing working for a loony like him? He is a loony, isn't he?'

'He's okay,' said Damian. 'I like him. He pays well.' He laughed. 'I like him even and he is a Brit. There's something about him that I like. He knows when a person does something well. That's good. There aren't too many people round who care if you do things well. They want you to do them fast. That's what matters. Get on with it. Get fucking on with it and cut the crap.'

Jack didn't say a word, just stood and looked at Damian sitting there staring out at the sea. Play it by ear, Manus had said, he may need re-activation.

'I want to build a boat one day.'

'Oh.'

'I have her in my mind's eye. A beautiful wooden hull. A sailing boat.'

'A sailing boat?'

'Yeah. I've spent too much of my life on those dirty, noisy fishing boats. Engines, oil, fumes. I want to be able to go out there on my own, with the silence. Ever seen a hooker?'

'Yes.'

'That's a beautiful boat. Something like a hooker. Smaller of course. Down round Achill they make this . . . oh, about a twenty-footer. A yawl, one big sail. I've thought it might be more practical, but I prefer the hooker. So.' He looked up at Jack suddenly and grinned.

'We'll get this station into working order. And then we'll start on my boat. We have it worked out. A gleoiteog. That more or less is the same shape as the hooker, only small.'

'You mean. . . ?'

'You see the goods shed up at the far end of the platform. He says we can build it there. There'll never be any goods for storing here. It's ideal. We'll be able to run the station between us and build the boat. No problems.'

'You've gone loony too. It must be infectious.'

'Where's the harm? I thought about it for a while when he asked me to work for him. I thought then . . . I have to believe in him. I turned it over in my mind for several days. Where's the harm in believing? That's what I thought. I like him.'

Jack laughed.

Damian put his hat on and stood up.

'You can laugh all you want,' he said. 'I'll go and get him. He can show you the box.'

He strolled away from Jack along the platform.

He may need re-activation, Jack heard Manus' voice in his ear. Re-activation . . . hell. He needed dumping.

He sat down on the step to wait. The warm smell of the sawdust tickled in his nose.

What would Manus do?

His methods were quite direct. That was one of the things Jack admired about him. I suffer from some kind of middle-class furtiveness, he thought, scratching his nose. The ground-work has been done there, sonny Jim, Manus had said. All you have to do is re-activate. . . .

'Ah shit,' Jack said aloud.

Those Donegal guys are a bunch of lazy bums. They'll do what they're told but they have no drive. You have to keep behind them the whole time. Nag. Get up there, Jack old son, and nag.

What he hadn't figured on though was the loony factor. 'Shit,' he said again.

Damian came out of the house and walked towards him.

'He's not up to it.'

Jack stood up. 'What's the matter with him?'

Damian shook his head.

'Sometimes he just lays there with his eyes shut. Tell him to go away and come back another time, he said. He doesn't mean any harm. He'll maybe at himself again in an hour, ten minutes, tomorrow. Come back tomorrow . . . and bring your mother.'

'My mother?'

'Yeah. He said bring your mother.'

Jack laughed. 'Like hell I will.'

'Suit yourself. I'm just telling you what he said.'

'Listen here, Damian, you know damn well I didn't come here to see him or his signal box. Manus said to contact you.'

Damian looked at him without speaking. After a moment or two he pulled his hat off again. The wind moved his hair.

'I'm going to make him a cup of coffee,' he said. 'I'll see you round.'

He turned back towards the house.

'What sort of a boat was it you said you were going to build?'

He kept walking. 'A gleoiteog.'

He reached the door into the house before he spoke again. 'I'll be in Kelly's Bar at eight.' He waved his hat at Jack and went into the house.

*

When Jack got back to the house, Helen was standing in the yard, outside the kitchen door winding up the old gramophone. He knew she must have been messing around in his room.

'Hello,' she said as he came in the gate.

The handle creaked as she turned it.

'What are you doing with that old thing?'

'Mary Heron rang about an hour ago to remind me that I'm supposed to be helping her with the white elephant stall at the ICA jumble sale next week. I had forgotten. Oh God, I forget so much. Even if I write things down, I forget to look. I'd forgotten all about this until I found it in your room.'

'Well that's a white elephant all right. No one's going to buy that.'

'Someone without electricity might love it.'

'Don't be daft, mother. Everyone's got electricity.'

She took a record out of a cardboard box on the table beside the machine and put it on the turntable. She pushed a switch and slowly the black disc began to revolve. Carefully she placed the needle in its shiny metal pickup on the edge of the record. For a moment there was a whining and then, slightly harsh but rhythmic, the sound of a dance band. She stood quite still and listened.

Why do you whisper green grass – gravel voice – *why tell the trees –*

'Someone will buy it. You'll see. Lots of records and two boxes of needles. I wonder if you can buy those needles nowadays.'

What ain't so –

– 'Look.' She twiddled a knob on the side of the machine. 'Those little shutters make it louder and softer. Listen.'

Whispering grass – the sound rose – *the trees don't* – and fell – *need to know.*

'I used to spend all my pocket money on records. They broke very easily. It's amazing there are so many left really.'

The gravelly voice battered around the yard. Quite incongruous.

'We could dance.' She did a little experimental twirl. 'Oh God, your father was a terrible dancer. He used to get all embarrassed when he danced and sort of seize up. The Ink Spots they were called. I suppose they must have been black. They sound black don't they?'

She twiddled the shutters again. The singer was talking now in a very black voice.

'Charlie Kennedy was the great dancer. It was such fun dancing with him. He could do anything. He used to practise steps that he saw on the films. The others stood on your toes or counted to themselves. He was great though. I wonder what ever happened to Charlie?'

'He changed his name and became Gene Kelly.'

'He was a divinity student, I think. Yes. He's probably a bishop by now. A dancing bishop.'

Suddenly she leant forward and took the needle off the record. The black disc whirled round in silence.

'A dancing bishop in Matabeleland. Beautiful black girls with naked breasts and men beating drums. In the middle of them all Bishop Charlie Kennedy dancing away in his surplice.'

'Matabeleland doesn't exist any more.'

She made a slight face and then pushed the switch on the gramophone. With a sigh the turntable slowed down and then stopped. She took the record off and put it back into the box. She closed down the lid of the machine.

'How strange,' she said, 'that I never played it down all those years. It's amazing really that it works after such neglect. Put it in the porch for me like an angel so it's ready and waiting for Mary when she comes to collect it. Don't drop it. I cherish it. I really cherish it.'

He did as he was told. There was a pile of his old clothes on the floor of the porch. He put down the gramophone and picked up his old school blazer which lay neatly folded on top of the pile. He ran back through the house and out into the yard. She was leaning against the low wall staring at the distant sea.

'Look here,' he said, waving the blazer at her. 'You can't give my blazer to a jumble sale.'

She looked round at him.

'Why ever not?'

'It's my school blazer.'

She laughed.

'You can't let anyone go wandering round in an old St Columba's blazer.'

'I wouldn't have thought that a thing like that would have worried you.'

'Well it does.'

'They can always cut the pocket off. It's hardly worn. Remember you did a terrible spurt of growing just after I bought it and I had to get you another one practically immediately.'

She put out a hand and touched the sleeve.

'It's very good material. The moths'll eat it if we just leave it lying around.'

'I'd rather you didn't sell my blazer.'

She shrugged. 'Okay. Okay. Take it away. Feed it to the moths. Do what you like with it. I'm going to go and have a swim. My head is full of unresolved thoughts and I smell of your old musty clothes. Come and have a swim.'

He shook his head.

'Do you good.'

'Dashing in and out of icy water never did me good. It's some sort of fantasy notion of yours that it does.'

'I'll bike,' she said, not listening to him. 'If you're not coming I might as well bike. Then I'll be so healthy I'll be able to shut myself in the shed for days and days without thinking about exercise or fresh air or anything like that.'

'What do you do over there for days and days?'

'Paint.'

'But why, mother?'

'Why not? After all, a long long time ago I thought for a time that the one thing I wanted to be was a great painter.' She smiled. 'That was a long time ago. I must have been about fifteen. Another fantasy notion.'

'Why didn't you? What stopped you?'

'I just didn't have the gumption. I didn't feel like suffering.' She scrapped at a piece of moss on the wall with her finger.

'Why would you have had to suffer?'

'I'd have had to uproot, learn how to be alone, wrestle with devils. So. . . .' She looked at him. The phrase 'wrestle with devils' had annoyed him, she could see that. He looked so like Dan at certain times, his mouth slightly pursed with displeasure.

'So . . .' she continued. 'Here I am. Here you are. Here we both are.'

*

It was downhill all the way to the shore, cutting across the village street between Harkin's Bar and Doherty's Spar shop. A hundred yards or so beyond the village the road became a track, pitted and hollowed by the wheels of cars and caravans. A gate in the high hedge of thorn and fuchsia led into one end of the caravan park, but the track itself meandered on between the hedges until it widened into a flat patch where day trippers parked their cars in the summer. The sea was hidden by hills of sand and only the low roar told you what to expect when you climbed through the bent and the neat piles of rabbit droppings to the top of the dunes.

The beach was long and straight, offering no shelter from the west wind that blew in from the ocean, whipping the sand into little eddies that scurried along above the ground stinging your legs and even sometimes whirling up into your eyes.

There was no one about. Wheel marks showed where a tractor had been down earlier in the day moving sand up to someone's farm. Criss-cross bird tracks patterned the sand near the water's edge. The sun behind a streak of cloud was moving at speed towards the rim of the horizon and, strangely, the moon, like a pale shadow of the sun, floated also in the sky. Helen had never been able to grasp the movements of the moon, but she felt quite honoured to be there alone on the beach with the pair of them. She gave a little wave.

'Here I am. Here you are. Here we all are.'

What a damn silly thing to have said to Jack.

How damn silly at the age of fifty or whatever to feel evasive, protective about the inside of your head.

She kicked her espadrilles off onto the sand. It had been so hot at times in the summer that to stand barefoot had been almost impossible; each grain of sand had seemed to scorch its way into the soles of your feet. . . . Now the sand was cool and slightly damp. She unfastened her jeans and pulled them off. Jack's indifference was slightly less friendly than Dan's had been. There was that element of contempt that prickled her. She dropped her jeans beside her shoes and began to walk towards the sea. Goddammit, the disease of parenthood was terminal. No way out round it, no hope of re-assessment.

'Nuts,' she said.

Five years before, five or six children had been drowned off this stretch of the beach. City children they had been, camping in the sand dunes. Sucked away into the innocent-looking sea by vicious undertow. She remembered the helpless sorrow they had all felt as each young body had been recovered. The County Council had put notices along the beach after that, warning people of the danger, but now they had become weathered, illegible, vandalised. She unbuttoned her shirt and let it fall onto the wrinkled sand.

'Why do you whisper green grass?'

The waves curled round her ankles. Not cold. For a few moments a million tiny stones, driven by the waves, beat into her legs and then the water became deep. You could feel the current pulling you as you lay upon the water. It wanted you to go towards the rocks at the southern end of the beach and then if you weren't careful away out into the ocean. The bodies had been washed in again about three miles down the coast, at the outermost point of the wide bay.

'Why tell the trees what ain't so?'

She lay on her back and allowed herself to drift. She knew for how long she could indulge herself in that pleasure before turning over and swimming strongly back into the safety of the breaking waves.

'Whispering grass, the trees don't need to know.'

The sun was quite indifferent as she sang, the moon as usual smiled.

'Why tell them all your secrets . . . deedeedee long ago?'

She was half-way to the rocks. A seagull floated above her, quite relaxed on a current of air.

'Whispering grass . . . oh no no no. The seagulls don't need to know.'

She turned over and swam back against the roll of the sea. After a couple of hundred yards she turned on her back once more and let the waves roll her in towards the shore.

'Oh no no no. Whispering grass. . . .'

Her bottom hit the sand.

She had judged it correctly, her shirt lay only a few yards away. She put it on and squeezed the water out of her hair.

'Whispering grass, the trees don't need to know.'

*

Kelly's Bar was dark and smelt of beer and a century's cigarette smoke. As Jack came in through the door he was wrapped in the smell, it crept into his pockets and up his sleeves, a total embrace. He got the notion as he stood at the bar and peered through the darkness that if the building were to fall apart at that moment, a solid block of undispersable smell would remain by the street-side. In the darkest corner Damian sat alone at a small round table. He raised his hand. Jack nodded briefly and ordered a pint of Guinness. He took the drink and carried it over to the table, pulled up a chair and sat down.

'I haven't had a smoke since I saw you last,' said Damian.

'Big deal.'

'Even my mother noticed. What's up with you, she said. No fag hanging out of your face.'

He laughed.

'She'll give me a medal, she says, if I keep it up for twelve months. I suggested she should make it hard cash. What would I do with your medal I asked her . . . knowing the kind she always has in her mind, smiling Jesus pinned to my vest. Aren't medals for to assist in the saving of souls? What do I care about damnation? She gets so mad at me when I say things like that. Upset. I shouldn't do it. She thinks I'm the walking personification of the ten deadly sins. Praying for me occupies a large part of her time.'

'Seven,' said Jack. 'There are only seven.'

'A Protestant point of view maybe. . . .'

'Ten commandments, seven deadly sins. Quite multi-denominational, I assure you.' Jack's voice was filled with humourless reproof.

Damian laughed again.

'There you are. I am an ignorant renegade. A bastún. She's right. Why is it that mothers are always right?'

One finger flicked away some Guinness froth that had been clinging to the gingery moustache that drooped over his upper lip. His eyes were amused as he looked across the table at Jack.

'I haven't noticed it,' said Jack.

'You don't live at home. When you live at home you find out these things. Mothers are always right. The truth becomes irrelevant when mother is around. Keep your head down and say nothing, that's what I've learnt. The odd leg pull and the rest of the time say nothing. Ah, she could be worse. I've seen worse. I've seen your mother down on the beach drawing pictures. I wouldn't have thought there was much to draw, but she crouches down on the sand like . . .' he paused for a moment '. . . some sort of a mad creature. Lost to the world. If you were standing next to her she wouldn't notice you.'

'She has bad eyes. Problems with her eyes.'

'It's not that. Lost is the word you'd use.'

Jack shrugged slightly.

'You don't say much do you?'

'You don't give anyone much chance.'

Damian stood up grinning. He picked up his empty glass and nodded towards the bar.

'I'm having another. Will I get you one? It'll maybe loosen your tongue.'

'I'm okay.'

'Live dangerously.'

Jack watched as he walked across the room and stood, his two hands flat on the bar, leaning towards the barman. Neat in his gestures, economical with his physical movements. Unlike his gabble. Over-fond of the sound of his own voice. Look at him there now, gabbling again as the black liquid crept into the tilted glass. The boy behind the bar laughed at something he had said, mopped the bar around the glass with a white cloth and laughed again. A bit of an opinion of himself. I wonder why is he involved? Family background? Never heard that. Conviction? Boredom? No, no, no. Not this one. Hate? He doesn't look the hating type. He looks to me like someone who drifted in and hasn't bothered to drift out again. Dangerous. They are the dangerous ones. No blinding commitment.

'There you are.'

Damian put the pint glass down on the table in front of Jack.

'Bloody bastards fleece you now for the harmless pint.'

'Thanks,' said Jack.

'Slap another tax on pleasure every time the country gets a bit low in funds. Drinks, smokes, books, the pictures, football. Squeeze another few dollars out of the buggers. Squeeze.' He laughed. 'There's one thing they forgot though.'

'What's that?'

Damian drooped one of his eyes and said nothing.

Jack thought for a moment.

'Oh. That.'

'Aye, that. It's a good thought that no matter how hard they try neither Church nor State can stop people doing that.'

'They do their best.'

'I reckon if they put their minds to it they could come up with some system. A computer implanted under the skin of every growing boy. Monitoring bad thoughts, sinful acts. At the end of the year you get a bill from Dublin. Five pence for a bad thought. A pound for self-abuse and a couple of quid every time you go the whole way. The country would be solvent in five years. I don't really amuse you, do I?'

Jack looked down at the table.

'Never mind,' said Damian, 'I amuse myself. You can't do better than that. Be amused by your own codology.'

'Manus . . .' began Jack.

Damian put his glass down on the table and frowned.

'What of Manus? The great God Manus. I can see you're dazzled by his very name.'

'You haven't a notion. . . .'

'And keep your voice down. Do you want everyone for miles round to know your business?'

Jack felt his face going red.

'I'm sorry,' said Damian. 'I speak a bit too quick at times. You shouldn't pay any heed. What's on the bugger's mind?'

'Well. . . .'

'Well . . .' Damian mimicked.

'He's not too keen on the way things are going up here. There's a sort of . . . ah . . . casual attitude to things. I think he's not too happy about.'

Damian smiled.

'He said to tell you he'd be up. He'd have to come up.'

'Aye,' said Damian. 'Let him come up. That would be best. No messengers.' He groped in his pocket for a moment looking for his cigarettes and then remembered. 'Anything else?'

'We need a staging post here. Somewhere stuff can be stored, adjacent to the border. Somewhere secure. It'll only be for a few weeks at the most. You're to find us somewhere secure. Quite quickly. No messing about.'

Damian nodded.

'How much space?'

'Quite a bit of space.'

Damian rubbed his finger up the side of his glass.

'About,' suggested Jack, 'the size of a goods shed.'

'Bugger off,' said Damian.

He lifted the glass and took a long drink.

'Think about it. You said yourself that no one uses it. Manus only wants it for a couple of weeks. You can see that the Englishman isn't around when we're moving stuff. You'll be there to keep an eye on things. Think about it.'

Damian put the glass down carefully on the table and wiped his mouth with the palm of his right hand. He didn't speak.

'What the hell are you doing in the Movement anyway?' asked Jack after a long silence.

'I'm not in it. I'm sort of alongside it. I'm not cut out to be a soldier.' He laughed. 'My mother's old man was a Connaught Ranger.'

He took another drink and wiped his mouth again with his hand. 'There was soldiers. He caught a shark when he was sixty-eight. Out one day in a half-decker between here and Tory Sound. I remember that.'

'That's. . . .'

'Listen. Will you listen. You don't speak anything but crap and you don't listen either . . . except perhaps to Manus. He lived with us for six years after my gran died. All the way up from Connemara he came. He found it hard to settle. She thought the world of him. She'd do more for your grandaddy than she'd ever do for me, my father used to say. She has all the books of old brown photographs . . . and his medals. He went to Dublin a couple of times, I mind, for reunions or something. My father used to take him to the train in Sligo. He'd bring his medals in a little black box. He always came back a new man . . . not just an old fogey telling his stories to the kids, because no one else had the time for him. You wouldn't remember his shark?'

'I heard the story. I didn't know it was your grandfather caught it.'

'Yes. Swan song.'

'But none of this is. . . .'

'Yes. Inside my head it is . . . relevant I suppose you were going to say . . . something like that. He used to talk. Maybe that's where I get my clacking tongue. Sit outside the kitchen door on summer evenings or by the fire in the winter and talk about the wars he'd seen, his old friends, the travelling, the great times they'd had together. India, terrible tragedies, happy days . . . all together like some kind of fairy story, only it was true. He would just sit there and let the brightness of his past catch up with him. I had all the time in the world to listen. And he'd talk about Ireland. You'll have to shoot them out, he used to say. They'll never go any other way. If you want them out you'll have to shoot them out. They simply don't understand the need that people have for freedom. People would rather be poor and suffer and be free. The English . . . he always talked about the English . . . don't understand a stupid thing like that. So you'll have to shoot them out, lad, and the quicker the better.'

'Well? Wasn't he right?'

'He didn't think it was right. He thought it was inevitable . . . like an operation without an anaesthetic, painful and possibly maiming. To be born Irish is a bitter birth, lad, he said to me. So many times he said that.' He picked up his glass and drained it. He held it out, the inside patterned with froth, towards Jack.

'Are you buying?'

Jack stood up. He took the glass from Damian's fingers.

'Manus doesn't like messers.'

'I don't like Manus.' Spikey orange lashes framed his hostile eyes. Jack shrugged slightly and went over to the bar. Guinness was written on the round mats placed at intervals along the bar. Three men played cards in the corner by the bar and from the carpeted saloon he could hear the sound of a girl laughing.

'A pint,' he said, pushing the glass across the counter to the barman.

'Only the one?'

'Only the one.'

There didn't seem to be any point in having the rest of Damian's life spilled out across the table at him. He had delivered his message. No point in wasting time.

'I talk too much,' said Damian, as Jack sat down across from him. 'Aren't you having one yourself?'

Jack shook his head. 'My mother is waiting.'

'Ah.'

'We eat at odd hours.'

'I like my meals at regular four-hourly intervals.'

'What'll I say to Manus?'

'How soon does he want this place?'

'Within the month.'

'I'll be in touch with him. You can give him that message.'

'Secure.'

'You said that before. One of the few words you have said.'

'I suppose we should try and like each other.'

'Remember the bloody nose I gave you?'

Jack nodded. 'I gave you one too.'

'You loosened one of my teeth.'

'Did I? I never knew that.' He felt obscurely pleased.

'It fell out six months later. Look.'

He rolled up his lip and Jack saw that a right-hand front molar was missing.

'I'm sorry,' Jack lied.

'No hard feelings,' said Damian. 'The girls like a fellow to be battle-scarred.'

'A sabre scar would be more glamorous.'

'True.'

They both laughed. Anyone coming into the bar at that moment might have thought they were good friends.

'I must go.' Jack stood up abruptly.

'Suit yourself. Thanks for the drink. I'll see you around.'

Damian picked up his drink and sauntered over to the corner

where the men were playing cards. He pulled up a chair and sat down beside them.

*

Helen looked at the four small water colours on the table in front of her. They were unframed, but neatly mounted on dark cardboard mounts. Scenes of sky and sea and bare hills. Light spilled from the sky, down into the deep blocks of shadows, lonely hollows, through the branches of the trees to become absorbed into the unkempt fleece of sheep searching for shelter behind a thorn hedge. Energy drained down, down all the time. The light troubled every object that it touched.

She ran her fingers nervously along the edge of the table. This may be the most ludicrous thing to do, she thought, but I must move now, somehow announce my presence.

A large canvas lay on the floor in the centre of the room. She painted that way, crouching down beside the canvas, leaning and stretching, the light coming above her head through the glass panes with which she had re-roofed the shed after she had moved into the cottage. Makeshift.

Exposure.

I have to have exposure now or become some sort of a mad woman locked into an ivory tower, pointlessly punishing myself for so many years of sloth. I must see them now in the hands of other people, see their eyes consider, explore, reject. Note the interest or indifference. Is it possible that for a moment they will recognise my existence?

Exposure.

She lit herself a cigarette. The tips of the fingers of her right hand were stained brown by nicotine.

'I want someone to buy you, even for ten pence off a jumble stall, and hang you on a wall. Another wall. Any other wall.'

She picked a black plastic sack off the floor and one by one she put the pictures into it. She folded the plastic into a neat bundle, her fingers in the end caressing the shiny surface of the bag as if it contained some dear and loving creature. Then she stood and stared at the bundle, hunching her shoulders up to her ears and letting them fall slowly again. She thrust the fingers of her left hand into the crevices between her collar bone and her right shoulder blade, probing to find the source of the stiffness that made sudden movement painful.

Decrepitude, she thought, creeping decrepitude. How stupid, how typical to leave exploration so late that decrepitude is setting in. She crushed the remains of the cigarette out in a saucer already filled with dead butts.

My whole life is makeshift.

'Mother,' Jack's voice called across the yard.

She hadn't heard the car.

'Coming.'

She picked up the black bag.

'Mother.'

'Coming, coming, coming.'

*

Dismal rain spread down from lethargic clouds.

'Where are the Cornflakes?'

'Darling, you said the other day that you didn't like Cornflakes. You threw them out. You said no more Cornflakes.'

'A passing phase. Today, I need Cornflakes.'

'They're in the press.'

He didn't move from behind the *Irish Times*. She sighed and went and got the packet from the press and put it down in front of him.

'There.'

'Mmmm.'

The cat, bedraggled from the rain and a night of entertainment, licked with vigour at his fur. When he was quite dry he would take himself to Helen's bed to sleep for a couple of hours.

She sat down at the table.

'Season of mists and mellow fruitfulness, how are you!'

The paper was a wall between them.

'Mists, yes . . . maybe it's mellowly fruitful in England.'

He turned a page, refolded, neatly, the paper. Newsprint in the country edition always greyed the fingers.

'Keats can't ever have visited the west of Ireland.'

Silence.

'Or was it Shelley?'

She stretched out her hand for the cigarettes.

'I always get them mixed up.'

Matches.

'A sympton of my crass ignorance. I regret . . . I really do regret that I didn't bother to learn anything at school.'

She struck the match sharply on the box.

'Everything seemed so irrelevant. Virgil's Aeneid and the isosceles triangle. Both equally. . . .'

She lit the cigarette and took a deep pull.

'. . . irrelevant. Litmus paper. What the hell about litmus paper?'

Smoke trickled from her nose and mouth.

'I did an exam question once on the Diet of Worms. I wonder what I said?'

Silence.

'Shakespeare, Yeats and Synge were as irrelevant to other people as litmus paper was to me. I noticed that much.'

The cat yawned exquisitely, exposing the pink roof tree of his mouth and the arc of pointed teeth.

'Any more tea?' Jack pushed his cup across the table.

'Do you think,' she asked as she poured, 'that Cézanne knew about Archimedes' Principle?'

'For God's sake, what does it matter?'

'I just have this feeling that everything should link up somehow. Form a pattern.'

'Do you always talk so much at breakfast.'

She poured the tea.

'I usually read the paper.'

She handed him a cup.

'It's a strange thing about men. They all feel they have this God-given right to read the paper first. Your father was the same. Untouched, unbreathed upon, unscrumpled. A male prerogative. Of course he paid for it . . . I suppose that made a difference. Sometimes he'd read me little bits from it . . . like throwing scraps to the waiting dog.'

Jack stirred some sugar into his tea.

'Father also said that talking to yourself was one of the first signs of madness.'

He went back behind the paper.

She smiled slightly, remembering Dan's voice as he had spoken the words, half-joke, half-serious to her so many times. A headline caught her eye and she leaned forwards across the table, screwing up her eyes to catch the small print.

'Oh dear.'

The cat jumped down from the draining board and walked out of the room.

'They've shot another man in Fermanagh.'

There was no reaction from the other side of the paper.

'Sixty-eight,' she read. 'A retired policeman. Letting the cows out into the field after milking.'

She put her cigarette down in her saucer and peered more closely.

'His wife was still in bed when she heard the shots. She got out of bed and looked out of the window. She saw him lying in the lane. Are you listening, Jack? I'm throwing you a scrap.'

He didn't answer.

'She threw a coat over her shoulders and ran out to him. He had been shot in the head and chest. She called for help. It was twenty minutes before anyone came. She put the coat over him and sat beside him and watched him die. She called and called. She didn't want to leave him on his own. Are you listening, Jack?'

'I read about it.'

'She must have been cold sitting there without her coat. Mustn't she?'

'If you would think mother. From time to time, just think.'

'Two men drove off in a yellow Ford Cortina which was later found by the side of the road two miles away.'

Abruptly he folded the paper and handed it to her.

'There's your thirty pence worth of liberal rubbish. I will now read the Cornflakes packet. It is just about as illuminating.'

He shook some Cornflakes into a bowl and poured milk on them. She watched. A sprinkling of sugar.

'I don't ask you questions,' she said.

He put a spoonful into his mouth. After a moment he grimaced.

'They're stale,' he said at last. 'That's what's wrong. Yuk. Stale.' He pushed the plate away.

'Probably.'

'I am grown up, mother. I don't have to answer to anyone. I am an autonomous person.'

She smiled slightly.

'Brutus is an honourable man.'

'Father couldn't talk to you either.'

'We just talked about different things, that was all. You are very like him.'

'I. . . .'

'Oh I know you wouldn't agree with me. He believed in the hierarchy of power. He believed that is was possible to impose, to keep peace by the use of violence. . . . He wouldn't have called it violence though. He didn't believe in God.'

'He went to Church . . . every Sunday off we trekked.'

'He acknowledged God in a sort of social way. He didn't believe in Him though. He preferred symbols to the truth.'

'I suppose you said all those things to him?' His voice was sarcastic.

She shook her head. 'Oh no. I didn't begin to understand him until after his death. I certainly never recognised his fear.'

Jack didn't seem to hear that word.

'He told me once that he sometimes thought you were a little simple.'

She laughed.

'Anyway I'm not like that. Not remotely.'

'Let's wait and see, shall we?'

They sat in silence. She put out her hand and took the lid off the pot and peered inside.

'The tea is cold. Would you like some more? I'll make some more.'

'Don't bother. I'll be off in a few minutes.'

'Off?'

'I'm going back to Dublin.'

'Oh, I didn't realise. . . . I hope it isn't because of. . . .'

'No. Bag packed and all. I have things to do this afternoon.'

'Do you want sandwiches? A thermos? Anything like that? Hard boiled eggs?'

'No. No need. I'll stop on the way if I feel like it.'

'Some fruit. I have some bananas. Easy to eat and then throw the skins out of the window. Bio-degradable banana skins.'

'Stop being motherly for God's sake.'

She got up and took her cup and saucer over to the sink.

'That's what I am,' she said. 'That's how I know I exist. I'm a mother.'

'Yoohoo.'

A voice shouted from the front door.

'Oh God,' said Helen. 'It's Mary and I'm not dressed or ready or anything. . . . Halloo. Halloo. Kitchen.'

The door opened and a small woman in an anorak walked into the room.

'I'm not dresssed or anything, Mary.'

'I can see that. Morning, Jack. I didn't know you were home.'

'Just a fleeting visit.' Jack stood up.

'Cup of tea, Mary?' asked Helen.

'No time to stand beneath the bough, dear. I've got loads of stuff to collect. ICA Sale, Jack dear. We've the white elephant as usual. Why I said I'd collect you first, Helen, I can't imagine. I should have known you wouldn't be ready. How long are you here for?'

'I'm off this morning actually. . . .'

'Lovely to be young again. No cares. Here today and gone. . . .'

'I have the stuff packed and ready in the porch, Mary. Why don't you take it with you in the car and I'll come down later on the bike?'

'My dear it's simply lashing.'

'A little drop of rain won't do me any harm.'

'If you really don't mind. Then you could take your time. See Jack off the premises. Dilly and dally. I have no doubt you'll dilly and dally. Won't she, Jack?'

'Darling, would you pack those things in the porch into the back of Mary's car for me? Sure you won't have a quick cup?'

Jack nodded and left the room.

'No tea, dear. I had the most enormous breakfast only a few minutes ago. I'm sure we won't have time for any lunch. He's looking well. So grown up these days. Didn't he have a moustache when he was last here? I get so confused about moustaches. If you really don't mind about the bike, dear, I think that would be best. Do keep covered up though. You wouldn't want to stand round all day in wet clothes. I'll fly away then. Must be there to marshal the troops. Don't be too long, dear.'

'I promise. I'll just see Jack off the premises and then I'll be right down.'

'Righty ho.'

She marched towards the door as Jack came in from the hall.

'Sorry you're off so soon, Jack. See you at Christmas, I suppose. Don't keep your mother hanging around for too long. I'll be needing her below. Bon voyage. Tooraloo, dears.'

She was gone. The hall door banged behind her. They stood in the silence for a moment looking at each other. He moved across the room towards her and put out a hand and touched her shoulder.

'Tooraloo, Mum. See you at Christmas.'

*

The rain stopped in the early afternoon. The sun came out and a small cold wind began to dry the village street and tease the leaves that lay in sodden heaps in the gutters. Liam the road man was supposed to sweep them up as they fell and take them away in his little cart, but nature's persistence always seemed too much for him and the leaves remained until the winter storms did Liam's work for him.

The hall was warm, quite stark, but cheerful. Mary Heron always refused to allow time to be wasted on paper chains and hanging decorations. On the platform at one end of the hall a dozen small tables had been set up and covered with coloured cloths and a number of women were sitting drinking tea and eating their way through plates stacked with sandwiches and home-made cakes. Helen was behind the white elephant stall.

Mary and I, she thought, are the true white elephants here. No one will buy us though. Neither useful nor decorative. That's not quite fair on Mary. She has her uses. She has drive, for what it's worth. This damn operation for instance, all these people pushing and buying cakes and useless objects they don't want, and arguing over second-hand cardigans, if Mary hadn't tooraloooed and tallyhoooed at them down all the years they'd all be safely at home watching afternoon soap opera or darning their husband's socks. Would they have been happier? We all spend our lives waiting for something to happen . . . and I suppose in the end of all we're probably quite relieved when nothing does happen. Oh God, I remember when I left the College of Art to marry Dan I was so sure that some magical explosion of love would occur, would shake me to the very marrow of my bones. I hoped then to be rattled into life and I was too damn lazy even to feel unhappy when it didn't work out like that.

'Wake up, wake up.'

Mary's voice poked into her head.

'You're asleep, Helen. Mrs O'Meara's been waving that tea cosy under your nose for ages.'

'I'm so sorry, Mrs O'Meara. How terribly rude of me.'

Mrs O'Meara waved the tea cosy again.

'Emmm . . . how . . . emmm?' She was shy and quite newly married and didn't really need a tea cosy.

'What about fifty pence? It's quite pretty. It looks as if someone made it by hand.'

'Fifty pence my eye,' said Mary. 'It's hand-made all right. Victorian. A real piece of Victoriana that. Beautiful work. A pound. What would you say to a pound, Mrs O'Meara? After all it's in a good cause, isn't it? You've all come here today to spend some money, haven't you? A pound.'

Mrs O'Meara, as if hypnotised, opened her bag and took out a pound which she handed across the trestle.

'Marvellous. Thank you so much. You won't regret it. You've bought a lovely little piece of the past. It might end up in a museum one day.'

Mrs O'Meara melted into the crowd, the lovely little piece of the past tucked under her arm.

'You are terrible,' said Helen, laughing.

'She can well afford it. That shop of her husband's is . . . what do they call it nowadays . . . a rip-off.'

'You're not too bad at ripping-off yourself.'

'Freddie always used to say I could get blood out of a stone.'

'I'd give anything for something else out of a stone at the moment.'

The old woman leaned down and pulled out a box from under the trestle. In it was a large thermos flask and several plastic mugs.

She picked up the thermos and unscrewed the top.

'A mug, a mug. Quick, get a move on. I see Father Quinlan heading in our direction.'

Helen held out two mugs and Mary filled the mug with what looked like effervescent water.

'I'm afraid it's vodka, not gin,' she said, screwing the top back on the flask again. 'Doesn't smell. It's cold . . . and strong.' She pushed the box out of sight with her foot. 'Down the hatch. Whoops.'

'Whoops,' said Helen.

'I thought our spirits might flag as the day wore on. Good afternoon, Father Quinlan. What can we persuade you to buy?'

'My house is filled with white elephants, Mrs Heron. Good afternoon to you, Helen.'

'Good afternoon, Father Quinlan.'

'I have strict instructions from Katy . . . just stick to the useful articles, she said, as I was leaving the house. So this year, Mrs Heron, I have to spend my money wisely. Jam, pickles, home-made biscuits. Katy will praise me when I get home, not scold. You wouldn't have Katy scolding me, would you?'

'Dear Father Quinlan, Katy will scold the Lord God Himself when she gets to heaven, so you'll be in good company.'

He smiled.

When he smiled he showed an expanse of rather yellowing teeth and his tired eyes gleamed for a moment. He was a gardener, and his fingernails were more times filled with earth and his finger tips rough and pitted with grubbing in the soil. In spite of Katy's most strenuous efforts he was frequently seen with the knees of his trousers seamed with mud.

'I spend most of my life on my knees,' he would smile and his eyes would gleam and his fingers would brush without much enthusiasm at the stains. His eyes wandered over the stall and rested for a moment on one of Helen's watercolours propped up against a tarnished brass jug. He put out a hand towards it. Helen turned away. She groped for the plastic mug and took a large gulp. Then she turned slightly so that she could see what was happening out of the side of her eye. She saw his black nails.

'Framed up and it would be a nice little picture. Who did that now?'

'I haven't the faintest idea,' said Mary. 'Do you know, Helen? There's another couple somewhere.'

'No . . . well. . . . No.'

'Framed up,' said the priest, holding the picture at arm's length. 'A bit of glass and a nice narrow frame. What do you think, Helen?'

'Yes,' said Helen foolishly.

'I don't see that Katy could make too much of a fuss about a nice wee picture of sheep and shadows.' He laughed suddenly.

'I'm sure I can find some suitable soothing text to calm her. And all that admirable jam.' He turned the picture over and peered down to find a signature.

'A modest artist,' he murmured. 'How much . . . ah . . . Mrs Heron, would you want me to be forking out for this charming picture?'

'There are two more, if you wait a moment. . . .'

He shook his head quite firmly.

'No. I am very happy with the one I have. If you produce two more I will have to make decisions, judgments. Also, Mrs Heron, confidentially with that little bit of sun, I want to get back to the garden. There is so much tidying-up to do before the winter sets in.'

'Five, father. Five. It's all in a good cause and as you said yourself it's a nice little picture.'

He took his wallet out of his pocket and handed her over a five-pound note.

'When it comes to raising funds, Mrs Heron, there's no one to beat you.'

'Get back to your garden quick now, Father Quinlan, and God bless you.'

He tucked the picture under his left arm, made a little bow towards the two of them and turned and walked quickly towards the door.

Mary put the note into the cash box.

'Where the hell did I put the other two? Do you think we can do that again? Ah, here they are. I doubt it.' She pulled the pictures out from under a pile of discoloured lace and propped them up against a couple of jugs. 'Freddie liked him. Did you paint them dear? Quite nice, quite nice. Perhaps I should have asked him for more. I like him. He used to come up and play chess with Freddie when he was dying. He'd chat about trees and things . . . fishing . . . all the things that Freddie liked you know. Of course you never knew Freddie did you? He had more time for him than old Canon Fergusson. That was in the days when we had a Rector . . . old Canon Fergusson. He didn't know a bishop from a castle. He played bridge quite well though. He used to want to talk to Freddie about God. I suppose he felt it was his duty or something like that. Freddie hated that. Silly old bugger he used to say . . . just because he wears his collar back to front doesn't mean he knows any more about God than I do. Poor old Canon Fergusson. He was a little dim. Could you call that blasphemy? I don't suppose so really, just a bit of arrogance perhaps. I don't suppose God held it against him. Do you?'

She took her plastic mug from the window sill and drained it. 'Bottoms up.'

'Does that gramophone work?'

Helen turned, startled by the strange voice.

'I'm sorry. . . .'

'The gramophone.'

He pointed with his only arm at the gramophone which was sitting on an upturned box beside the trestle table.

'Oh, Mr Haythorne . . . yes . . . it does . . . but you have to wind it up.'

He smiled. His mouth twisted up to the left and seemed to get caught in the scar that ran down his face from the eye-patch to the chin.

'Yes,' he said gently. 'I presumed you had to do that.'

'It is Haythorne, isn't it?'

'Hawthorne. Roger Hawthorne. I don't mind winding it up. In fact I'd quite enjoy it. Hawthorne.' He repeated a little sternly. He looked at her for a moment.

'I think perhaps I was a little rude to you the other day. Brusque . . . I. . . .'

'It's all right,' she said. 'It doesn't matter.'

'Of course I'd need some records if I were to buy it. Wouldn't I?'

'There are some. Not classical, I'm afraid. Look.'

She hoisted up the box of records from the floor and balanced it on the trestle.

'They're terribly old. My father gave me the machine when I passed my school certificate. 1947. Isn't that a ghastly thought. I did have some decent records, but they all seem to have disappeared. I suppose I must have thrown them out at some stage. Do have a look through these and see if there are any you'd like. There are several boxes of needles too. Every modern convenience.'

'Introduce me to your friend.'

Mary had the thermos flask in her hand.

'Oh yes. This is Mr Hawthorne. Mrs Heron.'

He bowed formally and held out his hand. Mary took it.

'Cold hand, warm heart. How do you do?'

'How do you do, Mrs Heron? I'm afraid it's merely bad circulation in my case. They say my heart is equally cold.'

She bent and picked a mug from the box. She filled it up from the thermos. 'A heart-warmer.' She offered it to him and then filled up her own mug and Helen's. He looked rather nervously at the liquid.

'It's not Eno's Fruit Salts,' she said. 'Down the hatch, man. Unless of course you're TT.'

Helen laughed. 'It's vodka and tonic. It's only recommendation being that it doesn't smell. So no one knows the sin that goes on behind the white elephant stall.'

'Thank you.'

'Personally,' said Mary, 'I'm a whiskey drinker. But there are times. . . . Mud in your eye.'

He smiled.

'Mud.'

'And if you're interested in the gramophone it'll be five pounds and the records two pence each.'

'Really, Mary. . . .'

'Take it or leave it.' She put her mug down and turned to deal with a woman who looked as if she might be about to buy a small oriental gong on a black lacquer stand.

'So, now you know,' said Helen.

He put the mug down carefully on the table and took a record out of the box. 'Spring will be a little late this year. Worth every bit of twopence, I'd have thought.'

'I think the records should be thrown in. After all. . . .'

'Embrace me, you sweet embraceable you. On the sunny side of the street. Deeda deedadeeda.'

He looked weird, she thought.

'This is a lovely way to spend an evening. The tune is in my head but the words escape me. Go back, Mrs . . . go back to your selling and leave me to wallow in vodka and nostalgia.'

'If you're. . . .'

'I am. Quite, quite all right.'

He was brusque again, very dismissive.

Odious, unpleasant man, she thought. How I dislike you. She moved up to the other end of the trestle, putting Mary between herself and the man. Let her extort what she can from you.

Bong.

Mary had just struck the gong with its padded beater.

'A fine mellifluous note. Much, much too cheap at a pound.'

A note changed hands.

Bong.

The new owner struck it again before picking it up and heading for home, to a better life now that she owned a gong.

Cakes and Biscuits were packing up, shaking and folding the white cloths with which the card tables had been covered. Home Produce and Flowers were counting money into a black tin box. Teas were still going strong. The rain was banging on the corrugated roof once more, bursting and racing down the roof and over the gutters and into the street. Women struggled into macintoshes and put up umbrellas in the porch and children were pulled roughly in off the street to the shelter of the hall again.

'Would it be all right if I were to check that the machine is in full working order?'

His voice was polite again.

'Of course.'

He lifted the domed lid and examined the turntable. He twiddled the knob that worked the shutters.

'Nice piece of mahogany,' he said.

'Things were made to last in those days,' said Mary. 'They hadn't cottoned on to the idea of consumerism.'

Beside Helen some children were dropping coins into a bucket of water. The handle squeaked as he turned it.

'What are we going to do with all this junk now, Mary? I don't think anyone is going to buy anything else.'

'We'll pack it all up, dear. I'll bring the lot home and put them in the cellar and roll them out again next time round. My dear, there are objects here have been on this stall for ten years.'

Helen picked up her two unsold pictures.

'I'll just. . . .'

'Take anything you like, dear.'

Track forty-nine. . . . Swelling fortissimo as he opened the shutters.

The children by the bucket looked round, startled.

It's the Chattanooga choochoo –

'Heavens.'

Mary clapped her hands over her ears.

All aboard

Wooohooo –

The children looked rather pleased.

It's the Chattanooga choochoo.

'Shall we dance?' He held out his hand to her.

'I. . . .' She propped the pictures up on the window. 'Why not?'

You leave the Pennsylvania station at a quarter to four –

A totally forgotten shiver happened in her stomach as she put her hand in his. Fright and then relief that you weren't going to be left alone smiling into space while the whole world danced around you. Foolish Helen –

Dinner in the diner –

He let go of her fingers and put his hand firmly on the small of her back.

Nothing could be finer –

Tentatively she took hold of both of his shoulders. Was that the right thing to do?

Than to have your ham and eggs in Carolina.

'Ca–ha–rol–ina.' He tilted his head away from her and sang.

Woohoo.

Everyone was watching.

He twirled her into the middle of the floor. It was sticky, she thought, her feet wouldn't slide, damp patches on the floor and Coke bottle tops, crisp packets. Not quite the Metropole ballroom or the Gresham Hotel. 'Whirl,' he whispered in her ear. 'Let's whirl. Let's show them something.' They whirled in spite of the sticky floor. It was fun, she thought. Such long ago fun. It's amazing he dances so well with his . . . disabilities. Rhythm. That was always the important thing. Rhythm. He must have been good when he was . . . when he was . . . I suppose at some time he was whole. People's pink faces smiled.

Won't you choochoo me home.

'Thank you,' he said and bowed quite formally.

Several people clapped.

'Avanti, avanti,' shouted Mary from beside the gramophone. She put another record on the turntable and gently lowered the needle.

Plinky plonky plinky plonky –

'Mmmm,' said the man, taking hold of her back again. His eye smiled at her.

Why do you whisper green grass?

'Why indeed,' he said.

Why tell the trees what ain't so? Some of the children began to dance as well, swaying slowly on their own.

Whispering grass —

'I know this one,' shouted Mrs Walsh, sweeping the floor by Home Produce. 'This brings me back. The trees don't need to know,' she shouted.

Oh no.

'Remember the Ink Spots.'

'Mr Hawthorne. . . .'

'Why tell them all your secrets? Call me Roger.'

'I haven't got any secrets.'

He smiled. 'I don't believe that. You have the most secretive face I have ever seen. Cool, private. Hiding things.'

'You dance well.'

Then she blushed. What a cow-like thing to say. His hand pressed her back for a moment.

'I used to dance a lot.'

Don't tell it to the trees or they will tell the birds and bees and everyone will know because you told the babbling —

'1944.'

He laughed.

Tree . . . ee . . . eeoooeeooee — slower — *and oooeeooee —*

'Oooeeoooeee,' crooned one of the children and the record stopped turning.

He let go of Helen and turned away. He walked quickly to the white elephant stall, just leaving her there standing in the middle of the hall.

'I'll have it,' he said to Mary. He pulled a wallet out of his pocket and produced two five-pound notes. He handed her the money.

'Here. That's what I'll give you.'

'Too much,' she said surprisingly. 'Give me seven.'

'Take it.' He pushed the money into her hand. 'I'll go and get my car. It's down by the hotel. If someone could. . . .'

'That's all right. One of the boys will carry it out for you. Wait a while though till the rain eases off. You'll drown in that.'

He shook his head and walked away towards the door.

'Fifty-seven pounds twenty-six pence.'

She put the money into the cash box.

She repeated the figure to Helen as she arrived beside her.

'Great.'

'It must be a record. It just shows the quality of our white elephants.'

'Or perhaps that our customers have more money than sense.'

Mary laughed.

'Vodka all gone. Let's clear up as quickly as we can and get home. Hot bath. Feet up. Here you, Kevin . . . it is Kevin, isn't it. . . ? Carry that machine out to Mr Hawthorne. He's gone to get his car. And the records. Don't drop it for heaven's sake . . . and don't let those records get wet.'

Helen took the folded plastic bag out of the coat pocket and carefully put the two pictures back into it.

'Mad as a hatter,' said Mary.

'Who?'

'That railway station man.'

'A grumpy bear, I'd have said. Mother had one of these. I always thought they were lovely.' She was folding a green velvet bridge cloth with gold tassels at each corner. 'I stole it once and wore it to a fancy-dress party. Wrapped round me like a cloak. I felt so rich. I spilled something on it, lemonade . . . something like that. There were ructions.'

She put it into the box they were filling.

'I suppose people don't play bridge with such formality any longer.'

'In and out of hospitals for years. Reggie and Anne know his people. He's been a thorn in their flesh for years. He buys railway stations.'

'A fairly harmless thing to do, I'd have thought.'

'One thing leads to another.'

Helen laughed. 'Don't be silly, Mary. He's a harmless bad-tempered crank. You're making him sound as if he were a homicidal maniac.'

'You just never know, dear, with the deranged when something terrible may bubble up to the surface. His family consider him to be deranged. Norfolk or somewhere like that they come from. There, I think we've done enough, dear. The others can cope with the final clearing-up. Just let me dispose of the cash and I'll drive you home.'

'I have the bike, thanks.'

'You'll get wet.'

'No matter.'

'Rain never hurt anyone.'

'So they say.'

'Run along then, dear, and thank you. See you soon. Tooraloo.'

'See you soon.'

*

Helen tied a scarf around her head in the doorway before stepping out into the rain. Dismal chiaroscuro street disfigured by prosperity. What a dismal thing to think. What nobility is there in the picturesque hovel? A horn hooted as she stepped into the road. Patience, she muttered. Her bike was leaning against a concrete lamp standard. Should I get a flashy new one? Gears? Thin wheels? All that sort of thing? Keep up with the times. Or keep old faithful forever.

Old faithful, we'll roam the range together.

The horn hooted again.

Old faithful, in every kind of weather.

Old faithful never knew about the North West of Ireland, that was for sure.

Damn! Hole in a sole and water seeping . . . now that was one of the world's most unpleasant sensations. Water seeping across the sole of the foot, clammy tights, cold, squelch.

'Squelch.'

'I've been blowing the horn at you for two minutes and all you say is squelch.'

He lent over awkwardly and opened the door of the car. 'Get in.'

'I. . . .'

'It's too wet to argue, just get in.'

'My bike. . . .'

He gestured impatiently with his hand. 'In, woman. In, in, in.'

Goodbye, old faithful.

She got in and closed the door.

'That's better,' he said. 'I thought we might go for a drive and then I'll leave you home.'

'It's not a very nice day for a drive.'

'If you want to drive any day will do.'

He did things with his feet and the car moved off.

'Perhaps you have other plans?'

'Perhaps I have.'

'I won't eat you,' he said gently.

'I feel I'm being kidnapped.'

'That's right. Only temporarily though. You don't need to be nervous. I handle a car very well.'

She felt her face going red.

'I'm not nervous.'

'This car cost a lot of money. If I were to pass out at any moment it could drive itself home and put itself in the garage.'

She laughed.

At the end of the village he took the right fork. This was onto a road that wound out through the rocky hills of a small peninsula. Water was spinning everywhere, blown by the wind. Wet trees squatted by wet stone walls, burnt slashes where the whins had been, glittered in the rain. No one lived any longer on this inhospitable headland. Sheep grazed among the rocks and the tumbled gables.

'The last time I danced was in 1944,' he said eventually. 'Thirty-five years ago, or thereabouts.'

'You dance one hell of a lot better than some I know who've been on the floor regularly for the last thirty-five years.'

'September the tenth.'

Oh God, she thought, he's going to tell me the story of his life.

'Do you mind if I smoke?'

He shook his head.

'Some people mind. They hate their cars reeking of stale smoke. I can't say I blame them.'

She felt in her pocket for the packet.

'They say nowadays that we . . . the smokers of the world are slowly poisoning all the rest. It's a dismal thought really. I suppose it's true too. I have tried to give up . . . oh ages ago, that was. My husband . . . late . . . my late husband gave it up just like that.' She clicked her fingers. 'I tried . . . but. . . . He encouraged me in every way . . . but . . . as you see I'm still at it.

My character is woefully weak.' There was silence. She clicked her fingers again to disperse the silence, but it remained. She put a cigarette in her mouth and lit it. The road had become very narrow, almost a track. Wet branches from the hedges scraped the sides of the car.

'I'm sorry,' she said, after a long time. 'I interrupted you.'

He nodded, but didn't say anything.

Maybe he is a homicidal maniac, she thought. But how efficient can you be with only one arm? One eye? Superhuman strength in his wrist, kicking, trampling feet? A rapist perhaps? I'd rather be raped than dead. No question. She looked cautiously at his face. She could only see the Picasso profile, the travesty.

How young he must have been on September the tenth, 1944.

'I was fourteen,' she said.

There was a gate in front of them. He stopped the car. He reached into the back of the car and handed her his anorak.

'Put this on,' he said. 'There's something I'd like to show you. I hope you don't mind getting a bit wet.'

'But you. . . .'

'I don't mind.'

He opened the door and got out of the car.

'It's only a couple of minutes' walk. You see when the wind is coming from the west like this . . . strongly from the west.' He moved towards the gate, where he fumbled with the bolt. 'Well . . . you'll see. . . .'

She put the anorak over her shoulders and got out. The rain and the west wind battered at her. The left sleeve of the anorak was tucked neatly into the pocket. She pulled it out and shoved her hands into the sleeves. He bumped the gate open across the grassy track. She walked beside him in silence. She knew where they were going. She knew the track like the back of her hand. Round to the right, down into the slight hollow where three thorn trees tangled their branches together. The wet oozing in through the soles of her leaking shoes as she walked. I will have pneumonia tomorrow, or at least chilblains. Up a steep short hill and out through a hedge of whin bushes onto the headland.

When they reached the edge of the grey plateau of rock he stopped walking. Without saying a word he pointed to a spot halfway between where they stood and the edge which hung out over the sea. They each stood in their own silence and waited. Grey is a most dismal colour, she thought. Dismal veils of rain. Dismal wind. I could be at home in a hot bath. She shivered with sudden delight at the thought of that pleasure ahead of her. Suddenly, like fireworks erupting, a great spray of water shot high in the air from a fissure in the rock.

'Ah,' she said with satisfaction.

'It only happens,' he said, 'when there is a strong west wind blowing. The water is thrust into an opening in the rocks below with such force that the only way out is up through that hole there.'

'Yes.'

He turned and looked at her.

'You've seen it before?'

She smiled.

'I've lived here quite a long time, you know. Six, seven years.'

'I'm sorry.'

'I didn't mean to sound rude. I thinks it's amazing . . . and it's ages since I've been here. Thank you for bringing me.'

He nodded abruptly.

'Jack and I used to bike along here when he was . . . younger . . . a kid. It's a good place for picnics. No sand to get in the sandwiches . . . and a marvellous view. You need a good day. Sometimes you feel if you screw your eyes up into slits you could see America.'

Great bars of rain moved in towards them, no America today.

'A good day,' he repeated.

'Perhaps you'd bring me back on a good day. We could have a picnic too. I haven't been on a picnic for ages.'

The column of water spouted again. Twenty feet straight up into the air, and then melted into the rain.

'Yes.'

He turned and set off back the way they had come at an odd jogging run. It looked as if it was quite hard for him to keep his balance. By the time Helen reached the car he was sitting inside it mopping at his face and hair with a handkerchief. She took off the dripping anorak and threw it into the back.

'They used to tell me when I was a child that rain would make your hair curl.' She slammed the door and wriggled her shoulders to keep the stiffness temporarily at bay. 'It never did me any good.'

He laughed. 'Nor me.'

He began to manoeuvre the car around. 'After all,' he said. 'Curly hair is a disease. A well-known fact.'

'You can't mean that all those millions of Africans are diseased.'

'Every one of them. The American blacks; all those Greeks and Italians with hair like corrugated paper, all, all diseased.'

'That just leaves you and me and Hitler.'

'Absolutely correct.'

The car was pointing in the right direction at last.

'That was what the last war was all about. The survival of the straight-haired. No kinks, waves, bends left on the face of the earth. Even the criminals, the perverts, the loonys, the murderers and the child rapists are to have straight hair. That's why I'm alive. I'm a straight-haired loony.'

The back wheels of the car were spinning in a puddle.

'It's just my luck to be caught in the bloody pouring rain, miles from home with a one-eyed, one-armed, straight-haired loony in charge of a lethal weapon.'

He began to laugh. He did something with his feet and the car moved more sedately forward.

Helen blushed and then she too began to laugh.

'I have passed a test . . . many tests . . . you know . . . and the machine has been adapted . . . at enormous expense. I'm really very safe in my machine.'

'It just slipped out.'

'My dear Mrs Cuffe, if I were in your position, I'm sure I'd feel the same.'

'Please call me Helen.'

He nodded. 'It's more helpful really when people acknowledge the disabilities of others. Mutilations, colour, madness, religion . . . whatever it may be. I have spent the largest part of my life among the mutilated. That for me is normal. I find the real world. . . . I had an aunt called Helen.'

'Oh.'

'My father's sister. I didn't like her much. She too was crippled . . . by her own sanctity.'

He swung the car out onto the road.

'Madam doormat, my father used to call her. Oh God, here

comes Madam doormat, and the temperature of the house would sink several degrees. He wiped his own feet on her when it suited him and despised her at the same time. So the name Helen. . . .'

'Doesn't appeal to you.'

'It has unpleasant connections. A long way back. We shouldn't allow ourselves to be influenced by such memories.'

'I think the rain is easing.'

'I thought perhaps I had discovered something new . . . a place no one had ever seen before.'

'That would be quite a triumph nowadays.'

'Yes.'

'It was really nice of you to bring me to see it.'

It was strange, she thought, how between one word and another the strange face could become a mask. It was like a grotesque sleight of hand; suddenly the magician removed all life from the puppet.

'Tobar na Diabhal it's called.'

He probably wasn't listening.

'The Devil's Well.'

There was silence between them for a long time.

'If you'd given me notice of your kidnap I'd have worn my gumboots. These shoes let in.'

'I never really know these things in advance. I tend to work on impulse. Anyway, here you are at home. Soon, you can be comfortable again.'

'Will you come in and have a cup of tea . . . a drink?'

He stopped the car by her gate.

'No thank you. I would rather get on home.'

He turned his head and stared at her.

She opened the door and began to heave herself out.

Ten years ago, five even, I would have been able to skip, skedaddle, now I heave and creak, like some ancient sailing vessel. Heave, creak.

'Are you sure . . . ?'

He still stared at her.

'I'm quite sure.'

'Will you be able to manage the gramophone on your own . . . to get it out of the car?'

'Yes. Thank you.'

It's like a drill, she thought, that eye, painfully penetrating. I'm so cold, drownded cold.

He nodded. He did things with his feet. She slammed the door.

'Thank you,' she called.

The car moved off and as it turned the corner she realised that she had left the plastic bag with the pictures in it on the floor by the front seat.

'Shit,' she shivered.

*

The door scraped.

Helen looked round from where she stood at the Aga, just taking the coffee off the heat.

Must mend that bloody door. Automatic, eternal thought. Useless thought. Roger stood there, the plastic bag tucked neatly under his arm.

'Excuse me for . . . I saw you through the window. It seemed silly to go to the front door.'

'Oh, hello.'

She still looked quite scrubbed after her bath. Her hair straight and very clean spread out from her head as she moved. Some nights after she had washed her hair it would be filled with static electricity and crackle and spark when she brushed it.

'Do come in. You're just in time for a cup of coffee.'

'You've washed your hair.'

'I had a boiling bath. You have to push that door quite hard to shut it. One day. . . .' She fetched another mug from the dresser and put it on the table, pushing the debris of plates, dishes and a few books up to the far end. 'Sit down. It's good coffee. Bewleys. A major extravagance. Instant makes me feel sick.'

Before sitting down, Roger put the bag carefully on the table. 'I thought you might be worried about your pictures.' He sat down. 'Yes . . . I'd love some coffee. I hope I'm not disturbing you.'

'Black or White?'

'Black, please.'

His hand lay quite still and heavy on the plastic bag, as if he were protecting it against some surprise attack.

'Sugar?'

She put the cup down in front of him.

He shook his head. 'I used to take sugar, but too many people wanted to help me . . . I don't know why . . . scoop it in, stir, take away the spoon just in case I dropped it on the floor, look at me with sympathy and concern. One day I just gave up sugar. Life seemed easier after that.'

Helen burst out laughing.

'How unkind of you.'

'Hardly that . . . self protective.'

'Would you like a glass of whiskey? Or some red wine? That's all I've got. Do have a whiskey. I'd love one myself.'

'That would be very nice. You're very cosy here.'

He watched her move to the cupboard, the sink.

'Everything at hand.'

Then back to the table with glasses, the bottle, water in a jug.

'Ship shape.'

She laughed. 'I wouldn't say that. I am famous for my lack of organisation. They wouldn't have me on a ship. Do you take water? Help yourself if you do.'

'A little water.'

She sat down opposite him and lit a cigarette. She flicked the match into a saucer already filled with butts and dead matches. 'How's your house coming on?'

Her fingers fiddled nervously with the cigarette. A thin string of smoke was caught in the light.

'The essentials for living are there. Your health.' He lifted the glass.

'Sláinte.'

'Damian has the box in working order. It won't be too long before we're ready. Then it will be up to CIE. I think we'll have to operate the level crossing gates manually to begin with, but I hope that after a while we will be able to tie them in to the box.'

'It was very good of you to bring that back for me. It was so stupid of me to leave it behind. The rain. . . .'

'I hope you don't mind, I took the liberty of looking . . . I hope that doesn't annoy you . . . your private parcel. . . .?'

'No . . . of course not.'

'Your work?'

She nodded.

'You didn't tell me you were a painter.'

'We haven't really had that sort of conversation . . . anyway I'm. . . .'

'You're a painter.'

She stretched her hand out across the table for the bag. But he replaced his hand, heavily, where it had been before.

'I would like to buy them.'

'Don't be silly.'

'After all, you were prepared to sell them at that terrible jumble sale. Why not to me?'

'It wasn't a jumble sale.'

'Next best thing. Why not to me?'

She shook her head.

'My walls are as good as the next man's. Better perhaps. Bare white walls crying out for pictures.'

'I would like you to give them back to me. I'd like to consider. You've taken me by surprise. I don't like that.'

'I took the precaution of writing a cheque before I came here.' He pulled the bag over to his side of the table and felt in his pocket. He took out the folded piece of paper and pushed it over the table towards her. 'I hope you'll forgive me and I hope you'll accept it.'

She stared down at it.

'Please.' His voice was very gentle.

She picked up the cheque.

'Why?'

'As I said this afternoon, I work on impulse. I like your watercolours. I want to hang them on my walls. For me that is quite simple.'

She unfolded the cheque and looked at it.

'A hundred pounds. I can't accept this. You're out of your mind.'

'So they tell me.'

He pulled the bag off the table on to his knee.

'I didn't mean . . . you can't possibly give me a hundred pounds.'

'I'm buying your pictures. That I believe is a reasonable assessment of their worth. I also believe that you don't know whether it is or not.'

She shook her head. 'I may of course be wrong. It's not very likely though.'

He took a gulp of coffee.

'There's no need to look so darn miserable.'

'I'm not miserable. I'm delighted. I really am.' She held the cheque out at arm's length and stared at it. 'I'll frame it.'

'I'd cash it first if I were you. I'll give it back to you when I get it from the bank. You can frame it then.'

'Yes. I don't know what to say. Have another drink?' She pushed the bottle towards him. 'Some more coffee? A slice of cold roast beef? Do have something.'

'No.'

He stood up. 'I'm going home. I find night driving a bit hairy. May I come back sometime?'

'I'm always here. Somewhere about.'

'I'll find you.'

'Yes.'

'I'd like to see what you're doing. Would you allow me. . . .?'

'Yes.'

He gave the door a sharp pull and the cat walked in, weaving through his legs.

'A cat. Your cat?'

She nodded.

'Well . . . really I'm his human being. You know what cats are like.'

'I'm glad you have a cat. I have very good relationships with cats.'

'Come or go,' she said. 'I mean . . . well . . . don't just stand there with the door open. The heat. . . .' She waved her hands. 'Come back in. We could talk a while.'

'No. Not tonight. I want to go home and play all those records and see how I feel. See what they bring back.'

'Masochism.'

'Possibly. Goodnight, Helen.'

'Goodnight. I hope you won't be found drowned in a pool of melancholic tears.'

'Unlikely.'

'And thank you. Thank you so much.'

The door bumped, scraped, screeched a little and was shut.

She listened to his steps across the yard. She poured herself some cold coffee. A freak?

In 1944 I was fourteen.

He clicked the gate shut behind him.

September the tenth, just coming to the end of the summer holidays. Time for dentists, shopping for new school clothes, warm vests, those terrible green knickers that matched the gym tunics. Time for squeezing your feet again into sensible lace-up shoes, feet spread by summer freedom.

The car started. . . .

He couldn't have been all that much older. Eighteen? Nineteen?

Drove away. The sound twisted along the road.

Only the wind then bruising the white walls.

In my whole life I have made two decisions. One was to marry Dan. I suppose that was a decision. I suppose at some stage I said yes. Pondered. Did I ponder? Or was I grasping at straws? I think for the record I will have to call it a decision. The second, of course, was coming here to this place, buying this house, throwing away all the detritus of the past.

I must be some sort of freak too.

She stabbed at one of the butts in the saucer with a match, impaling it finally like a cocktail sausage on a stick, then started on another.

The de-insulation programme has to begin.

The cat jumped up onto the table.

'Do you hear me, cat? Hear. Understand? I have to say it aloud. I am making a decision. Get that into your yellow head, through your yellow eyes.'

The giant step.

What was that game we used to play?

Forget it. Just get on with this decision-making moment.

The cold coffee was foul.

I could leave the issue untouched. I could continue to dabble in paint. Express myself to myself or whatever crudity of that sort is in my mind. I could sell the odd picture, get that satisfaction. It could be for ever a pastime. Pass time. If I could stop time, hold it here in this room. You may not pass on, old time, until I give you leave.

Oh for God's sake, even if I were to give up smoking and live to be a hundred that only gives me fifty years of rapidly passing time.

She stood up and remembering the game for a moment took a giant step across the centre of the room.

Cynical yellow eyes drooped.

Forty-nine years. Forty-eight.

I will become.

She went upstairs to bed.

When she woke up the next morning and looked at the moving shadows on the ceiling, she was filled with a joy that she had never experienced before, and likely never would again. Everything seemed so simple, so right. She lay and looked at the shadows and understood the meaning of ecstasy. Quite, quite abnormal for a person who had never allowed herself to be shaken radically in any way by emotion. For a while, five minutes, an hour, a whole morning, it was impossible to remember later, she felt liberated from doubt, from her own special wriggling worm of fear. Of course it all drained away, nothing could stop that happening, and she was left the same as she had been before.

*

No rain on Wednesday. A fine sharp breeze blew the clouds across the sky. Like a race, she thought as she crossed the yard, a mug of tea in one hand, the cigarettes and matches safely clutched in the pocket of her dressing gown. Boats, spinnakers full of wind racing across the sea blue sky. I will go to Dublin and buy myself a whole load of beautiful brushes. I won't blinking well stint myself on brushes ever again. I'll keep them clean, healthy. Build racks for them on the wall. Each one its allotted place. Fantasy of course. That sort of neatness was not in her nature. Anyway, she thought as she opened the door of the shed, the sky isn't sea blue, so it isn't.

She had been working for about half an hour when the door opened. She looked up from the floor, startled.

'Excuse me,' said Roger, as he came into the shed. 'You said I could come and see your paintings. Forgive me if I take you by surprise.'

'You certainly do. I haven't even combed my hair. I . . . I'm not. . . .'

'I can see you're not dressed.'

'I'm not even in my right mind yet.'

He smiled slightly.

'I thought if I came early I'd be sure to catch you in.'

'I'm always in.'

They stared at each other in silence. She struggled up from the floor, straightening the creaking knees.

'I'll go away if you prefer?'

'No. That's all right. I'm sorry if I was rude. You're the first visitor I've ever had in here.'

'Jack?'

'Oh God no. He never comes over here. I think he's frightened he'll despise my work and won't know how to cope with that.' She rubbed at the paint on her right forefinger with the forefinger of her other hand. 'He has his own way of looking at things you know . . . not a bit like mine at all.' She turned away and looked out of the small window at the end of the shed. In the distance a fishing boat moved against the rhythm of the sea, no smooth flow like the clouds, it butted against the sea and wind. Aggressive. Almost like I feel, she thought.

'He doesn't have to be involved. I would hate dutiful respect from him. I think I've probably hurt him quite a lot. He never wanted to come here. I think he felt quite orphaned as he was growing up.'

'It's impossible to protect other people all the time.'

She sighed and then she laughed suddenly.

'I spend a lot of my time over here in my dressing gown. I'll have to change my ways if I'm going to have a constant stream of visitors.'

'Why don't you go and organise yourself and I'll just stay here and. . . .' He gestured around the room with his hand. 'You wouldn't mind if I did that, would you?'

'I suppose not.'

She walked over to the door.

'I won't be long.'

'Don't rush. I'll be quite happy poking around here. By the way, I told the boy he could sit in the kitchen. I hope you don't mind.'

'What boy?'

'Damian Sweeney. I didn't feel like driving this morning, so he brought me over. I've taught him to use the pedals in my car. Sometimes I feel lazy, disinclined. I left him in the kitchen.'

'You do make yourself at home, don't you?'

He bowed.

She hadn't cleared the breakfast dishes, nor indeed the remains of her last night's supper. Time enough for all that when the light was gone, when her energy was low. Damian was sitting at the table with the cat on his knee.

'Good morning, Mrs Cuffe.' He stood up politely as she came into the kitchen. The cat, at his first movement stepped off his knee and onto the table.

'Bloody cat, get off the table,' said Helen crossly. 'Good morning. He eats the butter.'

'I think he's eaten the butter.'

Damian pointed to an empty saucer that might once have had butter in it.

'Bloody cat,' shouted Helen, clapping her hands. The cat jumped off the table and walked across the room past Helen and out into the hall.

'You probably don't remember me. . . .'

'Yes, I remember you.' Her voice was brusque. 'This place is in a mess. . . .'

'Yes,' he said. 'What of it? What's a bit of a mess for God's sake? You couldn't remember me. We've never met. I've seen you round the place, riding the bike and that, but we've never met.'

'You hit Jack.'

'That was years ago. We were only kids.'

'He came home in a terrible mess. It wasn't long after we came here and I thought, oh God, what have I let us in for. He was all covered in blood. Noses bleed such a lot. What a little bully that Damian Sweeney must be. A brat.'

'My mother felt much the same way about Jack. I'll say I'm sorry now. Better late than never.'

He held out a hand towards her.

She nodded and touched his hand briefly, then she plunged her hand into her pocket and took out the cigarettes. She opened the box and held it out towards him.

'Smoke?'

He was tempted. She could see that. He shook his head.

'I'm giving them up. Trying to, anyway.'

'Saint?'

She plucked one out of the packet and put it in her mouth.

'No. It just suddenly seemed a silly way to kill yourself. I think I'd rather drink myself to death, it's more fun.'

She lit the cigarette and took a deep pull. 'Do you see Jack at all? I never know who his friends are these days. He doesn't bring them home.'

'I had a jar with him in the pub the other night.'

'I hope . . .' she began and then stopped.

He waited for a moment. 'You hope what?'

She made a hopeless gesture with her hands.

'Would you make some tea? Can you make tea?'

'I can make tea.'

'I must get dressed. I really must. If you'd. . . .'

'Sure.'

'Will you be able to find everything?'

'Sure. Sure. Run along. I've been making tea since the age of five. I can open tins and fry eggs and gut fish and knit . . . I was ill once for quite a long time and Mammy taught me to knit. I knitted a navy scarf.' He laughed. 'I used to hide it under the pillow when the others came home from school so they wouldn't see it. She was the only one knew. . . .'

She paused by the door. 'What did you do with it?'

'I have it yet. I wear it in the winter. It's long.'

He wound an imaginary scarf several times around his neck.

'You go on and put your clothes on. I'll make a great cup of tea. Three great cups of tea.'

She nodded and left him to it.

*

It was strange, she thought as she scrubbed her teeth, backwards and forwards, she had never been able to come to grips with the up and down strokes recommended by the dentist, to hear other people, total strangers when you came to think of it, taking control in your house. Down the short flight of stairs Damian clattered domestically. She bared her teeth, grimaced into the glass. Yellow horse's teeth. If I stopped smoking perhaps? Across the yard Roger poked around through her entire private life, her being. She bared them again. Sparkling Doris Day? Too late. Yellow horse's teeth were more suitable to her age and station. He would be really shocked at the state of her brushes. Oh God, those awful half-drunk cups of tea, the old milk shining on the surface. At least they're my own, she thought, for the time being. One day maybe, I will have a mouth full of shiny Doris Day choppers. Keep them in a glass of gin beside the bed. But, after all, Mother didn't have a false tooth in her head, buried with her own smile. Runs in the family that sort of thing. Fingers crossed. She gave an extra scrub for luck.

Rinsed water round her mouth and spat.

Damian ran water into the sink, pumped in mild green Fairy Liquid and began to wash the dishes.

He looks nice. I wonder if he's mixed up in all that business. I suppose you shouldn't believe everything you hear. Nicer looking than Jack . . . not so buttoned up, sullen. Would sullen be the word for Jack's face? If Dan were still alive I wonder . . . I wonder? My eyes were always too pale to sparkle. Washed blue stones. Jack's eyes too, unreceptive. Are you receiving me? One two three testing. Are you receiving me, son? Silence on the air waves. A clatter of sound from downstairs. What the hell is he doing?

She picked up her comb and began to pull the night's tangles out of her hair. Damian turned on the radio. He really was making himself at home. Tchaikovsky's little cygnets heavy-footed in the kitchen.

'The tea's wet,' his voice called up the stairs.

'Thanks. I'll be down in a minute.'

She heard him open the back door and call across the yard to Roger.

The cat liked to sleep like a human being, tucked into the bed with his head on the pillow. He lay there, yellow eyes half-closed, as she tucked the clothes around him.

'If you sick up a quarter of a pound of butter on my bed . . .' she threatened. He wasn't receiving her either.

Damian had put cups and saucers on the table, milk in a jug, the fruit bowl centred neatly. No sign of debris.

'You'll make someone a good husband,' she said.

'My mother says no one will have me, so I may as well learn to look after myself.'

She sat down at the table.

'I'm not just a pretty face,' he said.

'So I see.'

She took a loose cigarette from her pocket and tapped it on the table for a while. The young man switched off the cygnets and stood looking at her in silence. Finally as if she had come to some immense decision she put the cigarette in her mouth and struck a match.

'It was really Jack made me give it up.'

'Jack?'

She wondered what he was talking about.

He nodded towards the cigarette.

She shook the flame dead and threw the matchstick into one of the saucers.

'He's never done anything so constructive for me.'

'I don't think he intended to be constructive. He just annoyed me.'

She sighed.

'I've seen you painting.'

'Oh yes.' She sounded vague.

'Up on the cliffs and along the shore. I sat and watched you once for nearly an hour. I wanted to come and have a look . . . but I didn't think you'd be pleased. It looked private.'

'Don't you have a job?'

'On and off. I'm working for him at the minute.'

'What . . . actually are you doing there? I mean you hear such mad rumours.'

'I have the signal box in working order now. Beautiful it is. Single line token block. Beautiful. You should have seen it before. It had to be refloored, new handles for the levers, new steps, completely new wiring, bells replaced. It's a gem now.'

'But listen. . . .'

'The token machines. . . .'

'Why?'

'What do you mean, why?'

'What on earth is the point of doing up an old signal box like that?'

'Station. The whole station. Soon we'll be able to work trains through the system again.'

'Don't be ridiculous, Damian. There are no tracks. There are no trains any longer. What are you talking about? Have you gone mad too?'

'He's not mad.'

'I suppose you could turn it into a museum. A railway museum. Tourists, schools, that sort of thing.'

'Will I pour you a cup of tea?'

'We'd better wait for. . . .'

Damian leant across the table towards her and spoke, almost in a whisper.

'Don't you go saying things like that to him. Do you hear me?'

'I. . . .'

'Just believe him, that's all I ask. After all, where's the harm?'

He sat back again and looked at her. She put the cigarette down on the table, standing like a little pillar on its butt end. She stared at the thread of smoke, at the neat crown of ash. Oh hell, she thought, there has to be disaster, unhappiness somewhere in all this. She heard his footsteps in the yard. She picked up the cigarette and knocked the ash into the saucer. Briefly she nooded at Damian. He looked relieved.

'You may pour the tea out now,' she said.

'How lucky you are.' Roger came across the room and put his hand on her shoulder, leant his weight for a moment on her and then sat down.

'Good tea. No other brew in the world quite tastes like Irish tea. I see signs over there that you are beginning to work . . . to find your voice.' He smiled slightly. 'Your silent voice.'

'Why do you say that I'm lucky?'

'Because you have eyes to see and the courage to want to use them. Maybe I should have said that you are unlucky. But I don't think you are a person who is looking for peace of mind. I knew a man once . . . a boy, I should say, whose parents called him Dieudonné. Imagine that. Imagine landing your poor child with a name like that. We just called him Don.'

'What happened to him? I mean how did such a stylishly named man deal with his life? With equal style I hope?'

'He died young. God regretted his gift and took it back. Arnhem, seventeenth of September 1944. Poor Don had the misfortune to come in on a glider that crashed. He missed the chance of becoming a hero. Very good tea, Damian.'

'I told her . . . Mrs. . . .'

'Helen. Please call me Helen.'

'I told her she should come and see the signal box.'

'Yes. You must do that. Come along any time.'

'Was that a parable? Was I meant to learn something from it?'

'A purely fortuitous reminiscence, I assure you. I haven't thought of the poor chap for years. It was just the name Godgiven . . . slipped . . . into . . . my mind.'

'Did you become a hero?'

He laughed.

'Alas. By the evening of the eighteenth of September I was just one of a rather large number of embarrassing reminders that God is not necessarily on the side of the British. We were all so convinced that He was. I'm not loving and forgiving, you know. I hate quite a lot of people . . . and I mourn the needless dead. You see, you haven't acquired a very cheerful neighbour.' Damian got up and went round the table. Gently he put a hand on Roger's shoulder.

'I think it's time we went home. We have all the down platform to clear. Remember? We said we'd do that today if the weather was good. Remember?'

'Good man, quite right.' He stood up and bowed formally to Helen. 'We burst upon you . . .' he said. 'I do apologise.'

'I just take a long time to get myself together . . . well, socially . . . in the morning. I'm glad you came.'

He moved slowly towards the door. A nerve twitched in the left-hand hollow of his neck. She could see it struggling from where she sat.

'All the needless dead.' He gave a helpless tug at the door. Damian stepped past him and pulled it open. He bent down to examine the bottom of the door.

'That's some big task you've taken on,' said Helen. 'Hating the living and mourning the dead. I don't know when you're going to have time to play all those gramophone records.'

Damian stood up. 'I'll come round one day and take a piece off the bottom of that door for you.'

'Oh, I. . . .'

'Dead easy job. No bother. Slán.' As he stepped outside he called back, 'Helen.' Just trying it for size.

'I didn't mean to be rude,' she said to Roger.

'I am aware of that. I think you should get together a portfolio of your work and bring it up to Dublin. If I could be of any help. . . .'

'Thank you.'

'You'll come and see the box? Soon. Come and visit us soon.'

He went out.

*

The days drifted past. The storms blew themselves out and the trees and the hedges glowed in the autumnal air. The evenings had a frosty sharpness and the glitter of the sun was tarnished by blue streaks of mist. After the hours of euphoria Helen felt a little bleak, insecure. The weather called her out of the house and she pedalled several times to the Devil's Well. It took almost an hour each way. . . . Soon, she thought, without too much hope, I will be fit and svelte.

She made sketches of the flat pre-historic rocks and the reflecting pools. Neolithic is such a good word, she thought, probably quite incorrectly nudging its way into my mind. It gives that feeling of grey unproductive rocks, existing eternally in spite of their unproductivity. The pools, large puddles really, quite still only reflect the glitter of the sky. . . . Lethargic birds stand, also still, waiting for a moment of lifting air, caring neither whether they stand or drift.

The house stank of size. She had to heat it in the kitchen and in spite of open doors and windows the smell was everywhere. She stretched and painted the canvas and cried with the smell and the reeking in her eyes. The canvas was beautiful. She stood looking at it, a delight of anticipation filling her. Then she went and had a bath and washed her hair, scrubbed the smell from every centimetre of her body.

She poured herself a glass of wine and went out to the porch to watch the last gasp of the sun. She rubbed at a geranium leaf and the smell burst out from between her fingers. The sea had that enamelled looked she loved. How can anyone bear to live facing to the East? Miss every evening this . . . in one shape or another . . . dramatic death.

The telephone rang.

Blinking miracles of modern science.

'Hello?'

'Mum . . . mother.'

'Darling, hello.'

'Hello there.'

'Is everything all right?'

He rang so seldom.

'Fine. How are things with you?'

'Just the same as ever. Beautiful weather. No news at all really.'

'I thought I might come down again for a couple of days. End of next week, perhaps. If that suited you.'

'Darling, of course it suits me. It would be lovely.'

'I have a friend I might . . . could he have a bed for a couple of nights? There's that old camp bed in my room. Would you mind? He's never seen. . . .' Crackle of some sort got mixed in with his words.

'Lovely,' she shouted. 'What's his name?'

'I'll be in touch before then. Let you know whether it will be Friday or Saturday.'

'Perhaps he doesn't have a name.'

Oh hell, she thought, why can't you keep your mouth shut. He'll hate that.

'Don't go to any trouble. We'll be out most of the time. He wants to see. . . . We'll amuse ourselves. Sure that's okay? Thanks a lot, mother. See you.' He was gone and by the time she got back to the porch the sun had set.

*

She got up with the light and worked for a couple of hours before becoming restless. She walked around the shed, avoiding looking at the canvas that lay on the floor. She had painted a layer of white into it with a short stubby brush then scrubbed at the wet paint with a cloth, dragging it across the canvas, clothing the bareness with a ragged substance. But, now, to her the white space was no longer inviting, she longed again for the naked canvas. She lit a cigarette and wandered across the room to look at her sketches pinned on the wall. She opened the end window to let in some air. She put the cigarette in a saucer and crouched down again by the canvas. She picked up the cloth and began to rub, harder and harder until in places the canvas began to show through the paint, faintly transformed in colour, but yet its own textured self.

'That is more like it.'

The sound of her own voice almost made her jump in the silence of the room. The cigarette had smouldered out. She lit another one.

'The first sign of madness.'

Again the voice startled her.

That was what she had always been told as a child. Talking to yourself again, Helen? The first sign of . . . you know . . . knowing wagging finger.

Helen loves the sound of her own voice.

If you can't think of anything interesting to say, Helen, it's better not to say anything at all.

My voice is too loud in this room. Keep the words internal.

Inspiration is a bugger.

Rising with the light was a rotten idea. Here I am, mind a blank and it's only ten o'clock in the morning.

Air.

My mind is blank, bleak like the scrubbed canvas.

How the hell do other, perhaps more mature people, manage to pin down the elusive bugger inspiration? Dan always said I was undisciplined.

Dan was always right.

She stubbed out the new cigarette.

God, how I hate the taste of them.

'One day . . . one day . . . one day. . . .'

She went out into the air.

In the house fat Mrs O'Sullivan was running the hoover over the sitting-room floor. She wore old tennis shoes without laces as she worked, to ease the pressure on her bunions. Helen put her head round the door.

'I'm just going out for a while, Mrs O'Sullivan,' she shouted.

The woman switched off the machine. It whined into silence.

'I feel like some fresh air.'

'It'll likely rain.'

'I don't think so. It looks gorgeous.'

'You should bring your mac. The man on the wireless said it was going to rain. Rain spreading from the west was what he said. I took my mac with me. No point in getting soaked through. Our Mary said I was foolish to take the mac on a day like this. Cloudless. A cloudless day. I said to her you never can tell and did you not hear what the man on the wireless is after saying? After all he's paid to know. Isn't he?'

'He's not always right though.'

'That's what our Mary said. Better safe than sorry was what I thought. I suppose you'll be taking the bike? They say that a regular spin on the bike is good for the muscles.' She switched on the hoover again. No point in carrying on fruitless conversation when there was work to be done.

Helen cycled along the upper road towards the old station.

The wheels snapped and crackled over scattered twigs.

Bones dem dry bones, she sang in her head.

Soon the furnishings of the earth would be gone, leaving only dry bones and stones, no clutter.

Hear de word of de Lord.

Someone had swept the dead leaves into a pile to the right of the station house. Smoke drifted casually up from the pile and there was a sharp smell of burning. She propped the bike beside the door and went into the hall. She walked over to the window of the booking office and looked into the room beyond. He was kneeling at a tapestry prie-dieu in the centre of the room, his head bent over his loosely clenched hand. She drew back quickly from the window, embarrassed to find him at such private practice. She moved as quietly as she could back across the hall to the door. A mist of smoke now gave the air substance. She hadn't really thought of him as a man who might pray. She had in fact never known anyone who had prayed with conviction. Prayer had always seemed polite acknowledgment of God's existence, quite formal. How do you do . . . goodbye . . . thank you so much for a lovely evening . . . see you next week. She moved out into the smoke and then, caught by its bitterness, she sneezed.

'Hello? Who's there? Is someone there?' his voice called.

'I'm sorry.' She went back into the hall again. 'It's only. . . .'

He appeared at the door that lead out onto the platform.

'I'm sorry. I didn't. . . .'

'That's all right. Come on in. I was just praying.'

He said the words quite unselfconsciously and held out his hand towards her. 'You are most welcome.'

'I felt I needed a change of scene . . . so I came up to talk to. . . .'

'That's nice.'

'Have a chat. I had to get out.'

'That's good. I'm pleased you came. Come in, come in. We'll have a cup of coffee.'

'I don't want anything.'

She passed him and went into the room.

'A drink?'

'Oh no thank you.'

'You must have something. I might get offended if you didn't have something.'

'Very well. Coffee would be lovely . . . at least . . . I'm not fussy, whatever's easiest.'

He moved the prie-dieu from the centre of the room, pulling it awkwardly across the floor to stand against the wall by the window.

'It was my mother's,' he explained. 'I'll just put on the kettle.'

He left the room and she could hear him moving in what she supposed to be the kitchen. Each sound came to her as if through an echoing cave. He struck a match. She wondered how he managed to do a simple thing like that. The gas popped. Water ran into a kettle, for a moment musical and then just broad splashing. He had hung her pictures on the wall. One above the fireplace, the other above a small Victorian desk piled with papers. They both looked new and unexpected to her in their somewhat prim wooden frames. His feet shuffled on the stone floor. The tin lid scraped on the kettle. She moved closer to the picture over the fireplace, to rediscover it in its new condition.

'You see,' he said behind her. 'They're good. I told you they were good. One day I'll bring them up to Dublin and have them properly mounted and framed. Damian made those frames.'

'Damian?'

'He has a great way with his hands.'

'I like them. I think you should leave them like that.'

He put two mugs and a bowl of sugar lumps on the table.

'It came as quite a shock seeing them there. I had resigned myself to never seeing them again. I don't quite know why.'

He opened a drawer in the table and took out two silver teaspoons. He put each one down carefully and exactly beside each mug. An obsession with symmetry was also one of the symptons of madness.

'I have only instant coffee, I find. Would you rather have tea?'

'No. That's all right.'

He went back into the kitchen. She crossed the room towards the other picture. The wet weight of the sheep's fleece seemed to burden it into the earth. It's okay, she thought. I thought it might just turn out like an illustration, but it does have an identity of its own. A little substance.

'Black or white?' he called from the kitchen.

'Black, please.'

She moved away from the picture feeling slightly guilty. 'Did your mother do the tapestry on the prie-dieu? It's beautiful.'

Old muted greens and blues. A unicorn gaily pranced through spring flowers. A girl sat under a formal oak tree plaiting her long golden hair.

He came back into the room with a jug and poured coffee into both the mugs. 'No, no. It's very old. It was her grandmother's, but it goes back a long way. French. She always had it in her room. I remember it all my life. It stood right in the middle of the room . . . bravely somehow. She believed greatly in prayer. Help yourself to sugar.'

She pulled a chair up to the table and sat down. She picked two lumps of sugar from the bowl and dropped them into her cup.

'She used to talk to God.'

'Do you do that?'

He was looking down at his coffee with a certain distaste. She thought he wasn't going to answer.

'No,' he said at last. 'I can't do that. She believed in miracles.' He laughed. He took a drink of his coffee. 'Oh, God, I hate that stuff. We should have had tea. She truly believed that I lived because she prayed. I'm glad to say she died before she . . . well. . . .' He waved his hand towards himself. 'She died. Maybe that was the miracle. You can never tell with God. He has his own way of doing things.'

'Why do you pray then? I mean, if you're not talking to God . . .? What? What are you asking him for?'

He pulled for a moment at the patch over his eye.

'I used to pray that I would die. I learnt however after a long time that I wasn't going to be given that . . . gift. My gift was going to be life. So . . . now . . . I ask for strength . . . grace. . . .' He looked across the table at her. 'Comfort. I pray a lot for comfort. It's no dialogue though. I batter his ears.' He laughed. 'You look quite bewildered. You shouldn't ask people such questions.'

She clasped her hands and looked up at the ceiling.

'From ghoulies and ghosties and long leggedy beasties and things that go bump in the night, good Lord deliver us. Amen. A very important prayer.'

'I went to Sunday school and all that, but I think we were politely informed that all lines of communication to God were through them . . . you know . . . the authorities. Be good and we'll see you through. Don't bother God, he has a lot on his mind. Later . . . I suppose about fourteen I became sceptical about the whole thing and then indifferent. I go to Church from time to time, for a sort of silly reason perhaps. I think the poor old Church of Ireland is a bit beleaguered at the moment. I don't suppose my occasional presence helps them much. I must say I prefer empty churches to full ones . . . silence is more appealing to me than hymns. What happened to your mother?'

'She was killed. Just at the end of the war. She had been to visit me in the hospital and a buzz bomb just came out of the sky.' He snapped his fingers. 'Like that. Somewhere near Victoria station. She was dead. Straight away. They didn't tell me for months. I couldn't understand why she wasn't coming to visit me. All the silly excuses they made. I knew they were lies, you know. Then when I was being shifted to the skin graft unit my father came in and told me. Very casually . . . one of those joke English scenes. By the way, your mother was killed six months ago, by a buzz bomb.'

He picked up his spoon and tapped it three times against the side of his mug. Three sort of exorcising taps.

'I laughed.'

'You shouldn't have done that.'

'What else was there to do but laugh? In another age I would have been able to cry. Now I would be able to cry, but then, I wouldn't have been allowed. It wouldn't have done.'

'Presumably your father was trying to save you pain.'

'Pain.'

He threw back his head and laughed heartily.

'I'm sorry,' she said. 'I'm not very well acquainted with pain. My life has been filled with minor complications and confusions, but very little pain. I think that might make me a little insensitive.'

'When your husband . . .?'

She shook her head most vigorously, but didn't say anything. He looked at her for a moment or two.

'I hope you are going to paint.'

'Yes.'

'Not just mess about.'

'Yes. I intend to take a portfolio to Dublin and see what happens then. There's so little time left. I've no one but myself to blame for that.'

He stretched across the table and put his hand for a moment over hers. He wore a gold signet ring on his little finger and the weight of it pressed painfully into her flesh. When he took his hand away she saw that he had left a red mark on her skin.

'Drink up your disgusting coffee,' he pushed back his chair and stood up, 'and come and see my signal box.'

'Have you a cigarette? I've left mine at home.'

'No cigarettes. You smoke too much.'

She drank some of the coffee. He was right, it was disgusting.

'Everyone says that to me.'

'You should stop.' His voice had a faintly schoolmasterly tone. He moved towards the door as he spoke.

'That's easy to say. I say it to myself all the time . . . when I wake up in the morning and feel like hell . . . when I look at the brown stains on my fingers . . . each time I cough. I'll stop on Monday I say . . . and then next Monday . . . after Christmas. . . . I gave it up for Lent once, but I thought I was going to die after about a week so I started again. I have very little strength of purpose.'

He laughed. 'So I see.'

They walked along the platform. Most of the grass and weeds that had pushed their way up between the flagstones had been removed. The broken panes in the windows of the station buildings had been replaced and the doors and window frames had been painted green. Between the platform and the white wooden fence that ran down towards the signal box a newly dug flower bed was waiting for the spring. A new sign on the fence was neatly lettered in black, Knappogue Road. 'We're going to plant bulbs in there. Just for a start. Red and yellow dwarf tulips. They'll flower quite late in the spring. We'll have to work out what to do after that. I like a station to have bedding plants, but it's an awful lot of work. Damian's digging another bed up by the level crossing. I've always loved those stations that had their names written in flowers. That's probably a bit too flamboyant for us. I expect we'll end up with something like heaths . . . perhaps even dwarf conifers. What do you think?'

'I don't know a thing about gardens. Dan never let me near the flower beds because he said I pulled up the plants and left the weeds. I was relegated to cutting the grass and burning the rubbish. I must say you have it all looking very nice.'

'Yes. It's coming along nicely. We should be ready for traffic in the New Year.'

She didn't say anything. She gave him a false bright smile and for a moment was afraid of his sharp eye.

'I'll go up first.'

They had reached the steps leading up to the box.

She climbed up after him. He pushed open the door and went in. She stood for a moment on the platform and looked towards the village roofs below them. Beyond the dunes a huge front of cloud was boiling up into the sky. Tremors of wind were starting to shake the empty branches of the trees.

'Everything is spick and span. First-rate,' she heard him say. She followed him into the box. There was a smell of new paint and brass polish.

'Have you ever been in a signal box before?'

She shook her head.

'This works on the electric token block system. There is only a single line here, as you presumably know, so the important thing is to stop there being more than one train in the section at any time.'

He looked at her to see if she understood.

She nodded. So far so good.

'The driver of each train has to carry a token . . . in some cases it's a staff. That's the most common. . . . You've probably come across them. But in this line it's a small metal disc. Look, it fits into this box.'

He showed her the slot in the polished box on the wall.

'When I put the token into that box it locks the section that the train is just leaving. No other train can go into that section without having that token. Then, this box, here, holds the token for the next section . . . understand?'

'Mmm.'

'When I take it out of the box, the signal levers for the next section are unlocked. Then I check with the next station that the line is clear. The bell. . . . There is a whole series of signals and replies. Listen.'

He pressed the bell twice. The two beats sounded quite clearly. She looked startled.

'It works.'

He ignored her comment.

'Train entering section,' he said. He moved to the signal handles. 'This one comes off danger now and then this. After she has moved into the new section, you put the signals back to danger again. It's absolutely foolproof. Of course, we have the level crossing here on the up side. That will have to be hand-operated, I'm afraid. We're a little behind the times here. Basic . . . but very simple to operate.'

'You might forget all these signals.'

'It's all written down very carefully in the rule book and I have the bell signals up on the wall there. If you are in any doubt at all you just refer to the book. Anyone could do it you know. There are never too many crises in a station of this size. The odd cow on the line, only minor problems like that. It's a good life. My station in Scotland was very similar.'

'You had a station in Scotland?'

'Yes, for four years.'

'Why did you . . .? What happened?'

'I had family problems.' He laughed abruptly. 'They wanted me to go and live in a home of some sort. Put quite a lot of pressure on me. They are strongly convinced that I can't look after myself.' He smiled. 'It's all to do with money really. I've never bothered them, you know. Tried to keep out of their hair. We haven't much in common. I'd been there about four years . . . yes . . . and they all descended one day without warning. A whole regiment of them. Brothers, sisters, their appendages, lawyers, doctors, all rabbit's friends and relations. They wanted me to sign things . . . to come quietly.'

He looked out of the window towards the distant sea.

'I never did them any harm.'

'What happened?'

'Well . . . I played them along for a bit and then did a bunk. I came over here. Out of the jurisdiction so to speak. It's much more difficult for them to get hold of me over here. I'm not really as much of a fool as they think. My lawyer's an old pal. School . . . all that . . . army rubbish. A good chap. He keeps them at bay. It took me over a year to find this place. It's good. I like it here. This is where I'll stay. They'll never dig me out of this place.' He turned towards her. His eye stared into her face.

'I never did them any harm.'

'I'm sure you didn't.'

'My mother left me a lot of money. That's the crux of it all. It enables me to live the way I want. After all that's why she left it to me. She changed her will shortly after. . . . She didn't know how things would work out for me. She told me that. She wanted me to be able to make my own decisions. It upsets them a lot. I do have to say that I get a certain amount of amusement out of upsetting them. Know what I mean?'

Sometimes his eye shone a brilliant blue, she noticed, sometimes it faded almost as you watched to a pale, tired grey.

'They can have it when I die. What's left of it. I think they're afraid I'll leave it to some absurd charity. Do you think I'm mad?'

'We all have a right to live the way we want.'

'That wasn't what I asked you.'

'I don't know the answer,' she said after a long pause. 'I mean, I don't think you are a person to be afraid of in any way . . . but, beyond that . . . I have to admit, I'm not sure where the boundaries are between sanity and madness. I mean anywhere . . . not just you. There is such a fine line between people who can accept the formalised madness of the world and those who can't. In Russia, after all, they put poets in lunatic asylums.'

'Here we leave them outside but don't bother to read what they have to say. There's madness for you.'

She laughed. No more tension. His eye lost its dazzle, softened in colour.

'You like the box?'

He gestured with his hand, embraced with the gesture the brass and shining polished wood, the boxes and handles, the telephone high on the wall in its cradle, the high standing desk with grooves for pens, the inkwell sunk in one corner and also, outside where the line had once curved away from the station, the curve slightly falling with the slope of the hill, the hedge that had been neatly clipped beyond which she could see the first signal standing at danger.

'It's beautiful. It looks just. . . .'

'Just?'

'Well, ready for use.'

He nodded and opened the door.

'It's the boy. Damian. He likes things to be perfect.'

He jerked his head towards the door, commanding that she leave the box.

'I've wasted a lot of your time.'

'Oh no.' She moved out on to the top of the steps. Leaves scurried along the platform. They descended the steps in silence. He grunted slightly each time his right foot thudded down onto the wood. They walked along the platform.

'I'm glad you said that,' he said.

Blue smoke twisted up from the chimney of the house. She could hear the sound of Damian digging at the other end of the platform, the rhythmic crunch of the spade entering the earth, the occasional clatter as he threw an unwanted stone out of his way.

'Said what?'

'About my not being a person to be afraid of. I wouldn't like you to be afraid of me.'

'I must get home, back to my cigarettes.'

'You'd better say hello to Damian before you go. Just a quick word.'

The tiny waiting room, she could see as they walked past, had a bench running round the wall and a polished table in the middle of the floor.

'A visitor, Damian,' said Roger.

Damian straightened up and stuck his spade in the earth. He wiped his right hand on the seat of his trousers and held it out towards Helen.

'How are you doing?'

She shook his hand.

'You're working hard.'

'There's no let up around here. The boss there would have had the pyramids built in half the time.' He winked.

'He's a slave driver is he?'

'Ah no,' said Roger behind her. 'Sweet reason is more my style.'

'Jack is coming up next week and bringing a friend. Perhaps you'll come up to the house and see them. Have a drink or something?'

Damian pulled the spade out of the ground and began to dig once more.

'I'm sure he'd be pleased.'

He pressed his foot down on the spade and it sliced deep into the earth. 'If Jack wants to see me, he knows where to find me.'

'Yes,' she said and turned away from him. 'Yes, of course. I'm sorry.' She walked quickly back along the platform, feeling a fool. Roger followed her. She walked through the hallway, past the window of the ticket office and out the door. She picked up her bicycle.

'He was rude,' said Roger, 'but then you were pretty silly.'

'I know. Fulsome, motherish, interfering, daft. We can't all be perfect.' She got onto the bike and sat, one toe on the ground looking at him. 'People say he's a Provo.'

'People say stupid things. Invent things.'

'In a small community like this, they usually know what they're talking about.'

'He never talks politics. I never talk politics. I have no politics in my head to talk. If he's a Provo it's his own affair.'

'They kill people.'

'Yes,' was all he said.

'Innocent people, children. Blow people's arms and legs off.' She thought for a fleeting moment of Dan. How surprised he must have been when those bullets hit him. No time for pain or anger, perhaps not even time for surprise.

'Before the British dropped us fools on Arnhem, they bombed a lunatic asylum. They were told that was what it was. They were told there were no Germans there, but they bombed it just the same. Better sure than sorry, I suppose some top brass hat said. The woods were full of poor mad creatures . . . just wandering, crying some of them. Lost. They were dressed in white sort of pyjama things. We all kill when we think it is expedient.'

'Is that true . . . about the lunatic asylum?'

'Oh yes, absolutely true. I only found out about it years later. I always presumed that those poor white creatures were part of my dementia. Sometimes I was conscious, then I suppose I was unconscious, but I always saw those white figures. Floating. They seemed to me to be floating. *Il Purgatorio*. You don't know how privileged you are never to have suffered.'

She blushed and kicked at the pedal of her bicycle. 'How do you know whether I've suffered or not?'

'Don't be angry with me. After all you said yourself you were not very well acquainted with pain.'

'I'm not angry. . . . It's just that so many people seem to believe that unless you have been through some sort of . . . oh God, what word can I use . . . hell, torment, anguish, you're not a whole person . . . you lack a whole dimension to your life. That's a form of arrogance I can't accept.'

His face was delighted.

'You are angry. You have such an untroubled face I thought perhaps you might never get angry. Anger is a very healthy emotion.'

She pushed off with her foot and left him standing there, idiotic grin dragging at his mouth. At the corner she turned and saw him still standing there grinning. She flapped a hand at him.

'Goodbyeee,' he called. 'Goodbyeee.'

*

Mrs O'Sullivan was mopping round the kitchen sink when she arrived home.

'My floor is only washed.' She looked with suspicion at Helen's feet. The veins on the backs of her hands bulged as she squeezed and bent the cloth. Helen sometimes had visions of her wringing the necks of chickens, rabbits, unwanted puppies even, her deep brown eyes quite calm as the hands moved. It wasn't that she was unkind, savage in any way, she just had all this power inside her, was unaware of her own strength.

'You're all red. It doesn't do to get overheated.'

'It was the wind as much as anything else, blowing in my face.'

'I've just made the tea. Will you have a cup?'

'Lovely. Thank you.'

'There's nothing like a cup of tea when you have everything red up.' She flapped the cloth out in front of her and hung it on the rail in front of the Aga. She picked the teapot off the range and brought it over to the table.

'Sit you down and rest yourself a minute. Let yourself cool off. Biking is for young ones. Not,' she plonked two mugs on the table, 'that young ones would give you tuppence for a bicycle these days. It's cars they want.' Mrs O'Sullivan's huge hand fished in the pocket of her overall for her cigarette. She always seemed to have a partially smoked one in there with a box of matches. She would have a few puffs and then carefully pinch it out and put it back in her pocket again, waiting for the next cup of tea. Then out it would come again.

'I was over at the station.'

Mrs O'Sullivan gave a deep and somewhat bronchial laugh.

'Now in the name of God what did you want to go over there for? Isn't that cowboy half-mad? You want to mind yourself with people like that.'

'I just thought I'd like to go and see what he was doing.'

'Curiosity killed the cat,' she said cheerfully.

'It's amazing. He and Damian Sweeney have done a great job. It really looks as if trains could start moving through it at any moment. All fixed up.'

'Now what sort of a person would want to do a thing like that at all? Half-mad is right . . . or whole mad. More money than sense.' She took a great swig of tea and swished it round inside her mouth before swallowing it. 'I mind well the time you could go all the way to Dublin in the train. You had to change of course in Letterkenny and Strabane. All the way to Dublin. I had cousins in Omagh. God when I think of the gas we used to have on them ould trains. The buses were never the same at all. And expensive. Holy God!'

Another little swish of tea.

'My uncle Eoin, that was my father's brother, he was signalman up there for near on thirty-two years. His heart was broke after they closed down the line. That's what they said anyway. He was too old then for a job on the buses. Some of them got jobs on the buses but he was too old to learn the new ways. You know what I mean? He lived for the trains. Loved the trains. Six months was all he lasted after that. I remember the very day he died. We had the Emergency then and nothing would do but my auntie Bridie had to pack her bags and away over to Glasgow to live with her daughter Alice. Emergency or no Emergency, said she couldn't face it here without Eoin. My mother and father begged her not to go. Sure as eggs is eggs, they said, you'll be killed by the bombs. She wouldn't pay them a blind bit of heed. She took a new lease of life over there, lived to be seventy-eight. Ah, sure you wouldn't remember them days.'

'Well, I do a bit you know.'

Mrs O'Sullivan crimped the end of her cigarette carefully between her finger and thumb.

'Maybe he's a spy.'

She dropped the butt into her pocket.

'Who?' asked Helen, surprised by the turn of things.

'Your man above.'

Helen exploded into laughter.

'What on earth would . . .?'

'I'm just telling you what they say. I'm not saying he is a spy. He could be a spy.'

'There's not much spying anyone could do here.'

'You find them everywhere these days. Tell me why else would he be here . . .? Messing around with that old station? Where would he get the money to do a thing like that?'

'I think he's quite rich and he likes trains. That's all. Obviously loves trains . . . like your uncle did. He's nice I think.'

'So they say. A gentleman, even an' he's had half his brains blown out.' She dipped a ginger biscuit in her tea and nibbled at the damp edge. 'Mind you what he wants to go getting mixed up with that Damian Sweeney for, I can't think. He's a bad lot if ever there was one.'

'He works hard.'

'He works when it suits him. He's all mixed up with . . . you know.'

She looked sternly at Helen, defying her to say a word.

'He keeps secrets from his mother. Now, the one thing I have to say about my lot is, they never keep secrets from me. Never did and never will. Open.'

'How do you know?'

'I rared them, didn't I? I brought them up in the fear of God and not one of them has ever set foot outside the marks; that's the truth. Mrs Sweeney gave those kids too much liberty and look at them now. Two in America doing God knows what, and Damian. Never puts his head inside the Church from one end of the year to the next. I said it to her, so I did, face to face, so I'm not speaking out of turn. Cissie, I said, you made your own bed, now you must lie on it. Too soft she was with them altogether. You know yourself.'

She gave Helen an accusing look.

'Oh dear,' said Helen.

'You know yourself.' Mrs O'Sullivan repeated the words triumphantly.

'Well. . . .'

'It's all in the raring.'

That seemed the end of the conversation. Helen filled up her cup with hot tea and retreated across the yard to the safety of her shed.

*

Next morning she walked to the northern tip of the beach. No one ever came here at all. Rocks grew up through the sand, grey lumps of granite. The odd cow wandered down from time to time from the unfenced fields on the hill. Sea birds lazed and strutted, hardly concerned by her presence. In the winter storms the sea lashed right up to the edge of the sloping dunes, but now the sand was still dry and bright with a tiny powdering of shells. She spread her towel beside a rock and sat down. She unwrapped her sketch book and began to draw, examining for her own edification the objects she saw around her: the strands of acid-green weed clinging to a broken razor shell, piles of discarded sand thrust up by some burrowing worms, the angle of a beak probing for food, the tight, delicate mechanism of a poised leg, the curve of rolling swell and the exact moment the spray burst. Page after page she filled. Behind her the rock still held the remains of summer warmth. She remembered having seen some notebooks of Leonardo, the explicit studies of a hand, fingers crooked, ridges of muscles running into the wrist; a bent leg full of power, the angles between jaw and neck, the tensions created even in stillness. After a long time her eyes were hurting, the fingers of her right hand felt as if someone had held them in a vice. She put the book and pencils down by the towel.

She stood up and pulled off her jersey and shirt and then her jeans and her pants and ran across the sand into the sea. She waded out over the breaking line of waves and then, falling forward onto the water, she swam straight out to sea, something that she normally wouldn't dream of doing, fear always keeping her within scrabbling distance of the land. She swam for a good six or seven minutes, thinking of nothing but the movement of her body through the water, the soft cleaving of arm after arm, the rhythm of her stretched legs beating, then suddenly frightened by her own courage she turned and swam back towards the shore. The rhythm was lost and her limbs felt the strain. She faltered, splashed, gulped mouthfuls of water. She moved from her kind of crawl to a more staid breast stroke. She turned over on her back and lay resting for a few moments, her eyes closed, her feet moving only enough to keep her steadily afloat. Having got back her nerve she began to swim again, feeling rather foolish. The tide was with her and she found she was moving quickly and calmly towards the beach. Once she found herself inside the arm of the bay she relaxed and began to enjoy again the motion of swimming, the weightlessness. What a life mermaids must lead, she thought. She shook the water from her face and eyes and looked towards the shore. A tall figure was standing beside her clothes. A hand went up to greet her. It was Damian Sweeney.

Bugger.

Oh God, she whispered a quick prayer up to the sky where he might or might not be watching over her well-being . . . don't let there be any hassle. No demoralising happening . . . Please God, I promise I'll buy some bathing togs. I promise I'll wear them, if that's what you really want . . . but oh bugger. . . . Dear God, why isn't he digging flower beds or turning table legs. The ground was under her feet now. She stood and began to walk slowly through the breaking sea. He bent down and picked up her towel from the sand. He shook it, both hands cracking it into the breeze, then he walked down to the water's edge to meet her. She stopped when the water was about knee-high and, catching her hair in her hands, twisted it into a rope, wringing the wetness out of it.

'It looks freezing,' he shouted to her.

She shook her head.

'I thought you were never going to come back. You don't swim well enough to go away out there. Were you not frightened?'

'A bit.'

She stepped onto the dry sand and took the towel from his hand. She wrapped it tightly round herself. It was cold now.

She rubbed at her running nose with the back of her hand.

'It's lovely,' she said. 'You ought to try it yourself.'

'I've more sense.'

She sniffed and laughed.

'I've no sense. It's a well-known fact.'

She picked up her shirt and jumper and pulled them, still attached, together over her head. She rubbed at her legs with the towel, thumping at herself with her fists to keep the cirulation speeding. She turned round towards him. He was jogging naked towards the edge of the sea. I hope to God he doesn't catch pneumonia, she thought. I bet he hasn't been in there for years.

Scrawny.

She dropped down on her knees and picked up her sketch book. Stringy. Jack wasn't like that.

He loitered on the edge of the water, his energy dissipated by the cold. His shoulders were hunched, his arms wrapped round his chest.

Jack was well covered, no sign of the framework.

He stepped cautiously like one of the wading birds across the first ripple of the waves.

Jack was pale. He took a sudden plunge across the waves and was down under the water. His arms worked for a few moments and then he stood up again and began to move back towards the shore. Suddenly in a great explosion of energy he rolled into the foam and leapt up into the air again. He twirled round, his arms high above his head and then down he went again, rolling again. Up he came and ran through the shallow water kicking great sparkling fountains up ahead of him as he ran. He ran towards her, shaking the water from his body as a dog does after a swim.

'Can I have a borrow of your towel, missus?' He put on a whiney child's voice.

She handed it up to him. 'You're all covered in sand. You should go in and wash it off.'

'Do you want to kill me?' He walked back to where his clothes lay, rubbing at himself savagely. She continued to draw as he dressed himself, as he rubbed hopelessly at the sand clinging to his legs and arms. He turned his back to her and stood on one leg and then the other, pulling on his pants and then his trousers. When he was dressed save for his shoes and socks he came back and dropped the towel beside her.

'What are you drawing?'

'You.'

He blushed suddenly and ran his fingers through his hair. He looked away from her out towards the horizon.

'Me?'

'Yes. Here, do you want to look?'

He squatted down beside her and she handed him the book. 'They're only sketches, but you can look if you want to.'

He looked carefully at each page. The trials and errors, scorings, shadings, heavy lines, light, almost invisible, wisps of grey. Stones, sand, wings, claws, beaks, sea, an arm, a leg, movement, stillness. After he had finished he handed her back the book.

'It looks like you're trying to teach yourself something. It's like a school book.'

She nodded.

'Do I look like that?'

'More or less. I haven't drawn a human figure for years. It was great to have you there miraculously . . . when I was in the mood.'

'I was up there.' He pointed up towards the hill. 'I couldn't think what you were drawing. There didn't seem to be anything to draw. I watched you for a long time.'

'You must have.'

'When you went in to swim I thought I'd better come down. I felt . . .' he blushed again '. . . if I'd stayed up there, it would have been like spying on you. So I came down.'

She smiled.

'Thank you for coming down.'

'What will you do with those now?' He nodded towards the book.

'I have a plan in my head for a series of shorescapes. It's just an idea at the moment . . . a wriggling germ, but I hope it will grow when I start to paint. I know it will.'

'Will you put me in it?'

'You'll have to wait and see. I'll have to wait and see.'

He leant forward and began to draw on the sand with his finger. He made deep grooves in the sand and then swept away the scattered grains as they got in his way. A small high-bowed boat, plain, heavy looking, sitting squatly down into the sea. A long bowsprit and one mast. His finger drew tiny waves and a mainsail filling with wind.

'Do you know what that is?'

'It looks a bit like a hooker. I'm not much good on boats, but they're very recognisable.'

'You're next best to right. A gleoiteog. That's what I'm going to build myself. I have a model made at home. Sails and all. To scale you know. I'll bring it round to show you some time.' He scrubbed the picture out with his hand. 'If you're interested, that is. You mightn't be interested. About this size.' He held his hands up to show her. 'A perfect model. I just thought you might. . . .'

'Yes. I'd like to see it very much.'

'I was rude yesterday.'

'Oh no, that's all right. I was a bit silly. Motherish. I forget sometimes that everyone grows up. That sort of thing can become so boring.'

'My mother's boring,' he said. 'But I wouldn't have thought you were.'

'Jack thinks I am.'

'She's nice, mind you. I didn't mean anything like that . . . but boring. She knits for the sweater people. The sweated labour people, I tell her she should call them. Sometimes I want to throw something at those clicking needles. I restrain myself. Jack's coming home, you said?'

'Yes. Next weekend.'

'Bringing a friend?'

'So he said. I thought at first it might be a girl. I got all motherly and excited again.'

'But it's not a girl.'

'No.'

'I suppose he does that quite a lot? Brings down friends?'

'No. I think he likes to protect his friends from me.'

He looked away out to sea. He looked, she thought, as if he were trying to see America.

'Did he say who he was bringing down?'

'I asked him, but I don't think he heard me. Why?' She gathered together the book and her pencils, the wet sandy towel.

'I just wondered. I thought maybe it was someone I knew.'

'Oh hardly . . . I mean . . . well . . . hardly.'

'Yes. Hardly. I'd better be getting back to my work.'

'You're mitching today.'

'I work my own hours. He's very reasonable like that.'

She stood up.

'I hope I didn't bother you.'

'Of course not. I hope you won't suffer any ill-effects from your swim.'

'Not a bit of it. Sometimes he's not well at all. It's quite hard then for the both of us. He gets these moods, like. You have to understand.'

'Do you think he'd like it if I asked him over for dinner one evening?'

'Aye. I think he'd like it. Goodbye then.' He took a few steps. 'Helen.'

'Goodbye, Damian. See you soon.'

He walked away up the beach, his shoes and socks dangling from his right hand, leaving deep footmarks in the sand.

*

For the next two days she lived in the shed, making short trips across the yard from time to time to make herself a cup of tea, boil an egg, feed the cat, who took quite unkindly to what he considered to be desertion. Bananas were useful, she thought. In Africa native tribes had existed for thousands of years on bananas; now, presumably, the glories of the sliced loaf and instant coffee had reached them. Monkeys too, very healthy, very energetic. A lot could be said in favour of the banana. Elephants even ate them with the peels on. She didn't bother to sit down to eat, just moved restlessly around the kitchen, watched by the disapproving eyes of the cat. The cups had brown stains inside them, a sign of true sordidness, she thought.

She remembered a moment with Dan. She blotted at the toast crumbs with a damp cloth as he sat watching, also, like a cat, disapproving.

'The really dreadful, debilitating thing about housework, domesticity, whatever you like to call it, is that over and over again you're doing the same bloody thing.' He hated that word. She only used it when she really wanted to annoy him. 'Bloody,' she repeated. 'You clear the table.' She threw the

cloth across the room towards the sink. The cloth landed on
the floor. 'You lay the table again. You wash the bloody
saucepans and then you dirty them again. You wash them
specifically to dirty them. You lay and unlay. Make beds in
order to get into them and crumple them. On and on and on
forever until you die ... or end up in the local bin, gaga,
incontinent and unloved.'

'Your problem is that you're a slut.'

'No,' she said sharply. 'I wish I were. If I were a slut I
wouldn't care. I'm just a boring woman with a boring sense of
duty. I feel my whole life is rushing down that bloody sink with
the Fairy Liquid bubbles.'

'I do wish you wouldn't use that word.'

'Bloody,' she said just to show that she wasn't intimidated
by him.

She laughed at the memory of it and went out into the yard,
closing the door on the banana skins and the brown stained
cups and the crumbs on the table and the cat.

The first painting was growing. The canvas had become a
magnet drawing out of her head an implacable coherence that
she had never felt before. Each stroke had its purpose, its truth.
The gaunt bones of the young man became a great stalk
growing up through the centre of the canvas, from its own
black shadow on the sand. She painted fast, the fear always in
her mind that if she faltered, looked back even for a moment
over her shoulder, Orpheus-like, she would lose her vision. She
spoke words to herself as she worked, meaningless jumbles of
sound, and sang snatches of songs that had become embedded
in her head for no reason. Over and over again the same phrase
would burst out of her into the room, until sometimes she
would put down her brush and give a sharp slap to the side of
her face to try and dislodge the irritation.

'What day is it?' she asked aloud.

No one answered.

She put down her brush and stood up. She stretched her
arms up above her head. Stiff. Every bone, joint, muscle,
whatever they all were, seemed to be locked hopelessly
together. Grey cloud pushed down on the glass roof.

'Thursday,' she answered herself.

She bent down and, carefully lifting the canvas, she carried it
across the room and propped it against the wall. She stood for

a moment or two staring at it.

'Thursday it is.'

No one disagreed.

She looked around.

'Bloody pigsty.'

She went over and opened the window. She emptied the ashtrays into a plastic bag and then threw in some tissues that were lying on the floor. Stiff back as she bent. Some dirty rags, and then some rolled-up used tubes of paint. Marginally less like a pigsty.

She went out into the yard and put the plastic bag in the bin, then she got her bicycle out of its shed and set off for the station. It wasn't raining, but the west wind was damp and squally. She had to struggle quite hard to keep the bike on the left-hand side of the road.

She didn't hear the car until it passed her coming round a corner. Roger put his hand on the horn in greeting and then stopped. She got off the bike and crossed the road.

'Hello.'

'Good morning . . . perhaps it's afternoon, I'm not sure. I was just going to call on you.'

'Snap,' he said.

He looked tired. The scars on his face were bunched together and shiny . . . somewhat grotesque. She felt suddenly guilty at thinking such a thing. She put her hand through the window of the car and touched his shoulder briefly.

'Go on ahead,' she said. 'I'll follow you back. I've finished a picture and I'd like to show it to you . . . well . . . to someone. I just suddenly thought I'd like to show it to someone. You seemed to be. . . .'

He nodded. The car gave a slight shudder and then moved slowly down the road. She turned the bike round and pedalled after him.

She brought him in through the little glass porch. Several of the geraniums still flowered bravely and the air was sweet. They walked across the hall and out into the yard.

'I've just been down looking for Damian,' he said. 'There was no sign of him this morning so I thought I'd go down and find out what was up. I thought he might be ill. He is usually so meticulous about everything he does.'

'I hope nothing's the matter with him.'

'No. His mother says he's gone away for a few days. Just took off last night. Odd he didn't say.'

'Yes. Odd.'

She opened the door of the shed as the first raindrops pattered around them.

'Rain,' she said.

She crossed the room and closed the window.

'I also wanted to see you,' he said.

The rain thickened suddenly, almost startlingly, rattling off the roof, splashing down into the yard. Everything in sight changed its colour.

'Gosh, we were only in in time.'

'For several days, I've wanted to come and see you. I don't quite know why I didn't come. Some kind of reticence prevented me.'

'This place is a pigsty. I'm sorry. Dan always said that I was a slut. He must have been right. I argued with him at the time, but. . . .'

'Are you going to show me this picture, or have you changed your mind?'

'Shut your eyes.' Oh God, she groaned. 'Eye. Shut . . . listen to that awful rain.' She looked at him. He stood by the door, his eye obediently shut. She walked over to the painting and lifted it up carefully.

'I wanted to see you,' he repeated.

'That's nice.'

She carried it across the room and put it standing up on the only chair. 'You can look now.'

She heard the telephone ringing from across the yard. She considered the possibility of leaving it to ring itself out, but decided against it. She pulled open the door and dashed across the yard. Curiosity killed the cat, Dan would have said coolly. The telephone had held no magic for him at all.

'Hello.' Puffed.

Crackle.

'Mother.'

Crackle.

'Hello.'

'Hello.'

Crackle.

Miracles of modern science how are ya.

'Mother, can you hear me?'

'Yes. Just,' she yelled.

There was a long crackling silence.

'Jack. Hello. Are you still there?'

She caught the sound of his voice again. A voice drowning in crackles. As it went down for the third time she heard the words, 'tomorrow evening.'

'Tomorrow evening?' she shouted back. 'Is that what you said? You're coming tomorrow evening?'

There was total silence.

'Hey. Yoohoo. Anyone there?'

It sounded as if someone sighed.

'Bugger the Minister for Posts and Telegraphs,' she said into the mouthpiece and hung up.

An old respectable umbrella of Dan's stood in a corner of the hall, ready for emergencies. His name was written on a thin gold band around the handle, in neat looping letters. He had always kept it immaculately rolled.

'Hopeless, hopeless,' she muttered to herself as she picked it up.

Roger was standing looking at the painting.

'Hopeless,' she repeated to his back. 'Do you know that the people are leaving this country in thousands because they can't communicate with each other. Thousands. What the hell is the point of paying to have one of those odious little black gadgets in your house, if it doesn't work?'

'I think it's a very remarkable painting,' Roger said.

She crossed the room and picked up several brushes that were lying on the floor.

She poured some turpentine into a cup and began to clean them.

'Why do you live alone?'

She rubbed at the handle of one of the brushes with a cloth.

'I'm not unhappy.'

Blue paint stained two of her fingers.

'That wasn't what I asked.'

'I like to be alone. It's funny how long it takes you to learn these things about yourself.'

She put the brush into an enamel jug where several others were standing and picked up another.

'I didn't discover that truth about myself until after Dan was killed. Up until that moment I saw nothing but my own inadequacies.'

She twirled the brush for a moment in the turpentine.

'I'm not lonely you know,' she said quite firmly, 'just alone. I like to live on the edge of things.' She sighed. 'Dan . . . he was very sane and well balanced. I suppose that was why I married him, I saw the lack of balance in myself. He . . .' she hesitated.

'Go on.'

She put the next brush in the jug with the others and turned round to look at him. He was still staring at the painting.

'He would have considered me to be irresponsible. He believed in structures and hierarchies, responsible involvement.'

She patted the pockets of her overall for a moment, feeling to see if her cigarettes were there. Having found that they were, she didn't need one any longer.

'Sanity. He believed in sanity.'

'I'll buy it,' he said.

'Buy what?'

'The picture.'

She burst out laughing.

'Don't be a damn fool.'

'I'm not. I want to buy it.'

'Well, I don't want to sell it. I intend to do a series . . . sequence . . . call it what you like. I see four in my mind. Then I'll take them up to Dublin. If I finish them I'll feel I really have something to show people. I'll be ready then. So. . . .'

' "So?"

'No more talk of buying. I don't want. . . .'

He smiled slightly as he waited for her to finish the sentence.

'. . . don't get me wrong . . . kindness, charitable offerings. I don't mean to be rude.'

He nodded. He plucked at his eye patch and she thought that he was going to pull it off. She didn't want to see an empty socket, or perhaps the eye was still there, threaded with red veins like the blind man who used to tap his way down the street where she had lived as a child. She wouldn't want to see that either.

'Of course you're right. Absolutely right. Look here, I feel like a drink. How about coming down to the village with me and we'll have a drink?'

'We could have one here.'

'No, no, no. Let's get out of here. Mr Kelly's insalubrious bar . . . or the Hotel? Take your pick. A celebration. Both are equally dismal. We could go further afield if you preferred.'

'The Hotel.'

'Right. The Hotel it is. Come along then.'

'I'm not really fit to be seen.' She laughed nervously. 'I don't think I've even combed my hair today.'

'You'll do.' He turned abruptly and walked towards the door. 'It's not the Ritz. Not even the Shelbourne Hotel, Dublin.'

He opened the door. It was still pouring.

'Hold on,' she said. 'I have the umbrella.' He was striding across the yard, impatient to be off on this jaunt.

'I must wash the paint off my hands.'

'Don't fuss. You'll do the way you are. Women always fuss so. Prink, pat, fiddle.'

'I am not going to prink, pat nor fiddle. I'm going to wash the paint off my hands. If that upsets you in any way, you can go to hell.'

She marched past him into the kitchen and turned on both taps with ferocity. He didn't follow her. He walked on down the narrow hall and when she came out of the kitchen he was standing in the porch among the geraniums.

'Did you have this built?' he asked.

She nodded.

'I've always had a vision of myself as an old lady sitting wrapped in shawls watching the sun set, in a porch filled with geraniums. The building of the porch was phase one.'

'Knitting?' he asked.

'Heavens no. Not doing anything useful at all. I don't see that my personality will change with old age. Staring into space.'

'A rocking chair?' he suggested.

'Perhaps.'

They scuttled out to the car through the rain.

'You don't like women much, do you?' she asked as she settled herself into her seat.

'I have observed their manipulations from a healthy distance. They tell lies.'

'Everyone tells lies when it suits them. Dan, who was the

soul of honesty, did. Mind you, he pretended he didn't, but he did. And you do too.'

'I don't tell lies.'

He slammed the car door and began to fiddle around with the keys.

'Of course you do. What's all this railway nonsense then? Trains? There hasn't been a train here since 1947 or some time like that. Over thirty years. There are no lines. No hope of trains. No more trains. Never.' He didn't say a word. He turned the car very carefully round and they drove in silence down the hill. She took her cigarettes from her pocket and put one in her mouth. He leant slightly forward as he drove, peering with care through the triangle cleared by the windscreen wiper. She lit the cigarette and took a deep pull.

'I'm sorry,' she said, as they reached the first house in the long street. 'I shouldn't have said any of that. I feel dishevelled, mentally as well as physically. I hope you'll forgive me.'

'There isn't anything to forgive. You have your right like everyone else to your point of view. I see my station working. Trains running through it. Goods. Not many passengers I admit. Most people have cars these days. Moving extensions of their homes; the same sweet papers on the floor, the same music, your old coat on the back seat, your own smell. Trains are different. Trains will run through my station again. . . . That's not a lie, Helen.'

He stopped the car outside the hotel. Macnamara's Hotel was written in black letters over the pillared door. Licensed Bar in smaller letters. Prop. Geo. Hasson, very small indeed. She got out of the car and followed him into the dark hall. The bar was empty. The eight plastic stools waited hopefully, the fire smouldered.

Beer and smoke and a smell of fried fish.

'Stool or table?' he asked her.

'Over by the fire, I think.'

He rang the bell on the counter and a voice called something from another room.

'I met your son here one evening . . . Jack?'

'Yes. He mentioned that.'

'He seemed a nice boy.'

'I don't think I know him very well.'

Mr Hasson came in, in his shirt sleeves. 'Well, well,' he said. 'Sir and madam. How's Mrs Cuffe? Well I hope.'

'Fine thank you Mr Hasson.'

'Weather changeable, wouldn't you say?'

'That's autumn for you. Unreliable.'

'And you, sir. All well? I hear the station's coming along nicely. What can I get you?'

'Helen? What would you like?'

'The young fella away back to College, is he? We don't get to see very much of him these days. Of course you can't expect young people to stick themselves away in a place like this. Back of beyond.'

'I think a glass of wine would be nice. If it's possible.'

'Now I wouldn't hold that view myself mind you. No better place to my way of thinking. Born and reared here. . . . Mr-ah-sir and my mother and father before me. Out of the soil you might say and back into it again one day. The young people don't feel like that at all.'

'Have you any wine, Mr Hasson? I think we'd like a bottle if you have one.'

'Away to Dublin they go the minute their ears are dry. I have a son in Saudia Araby. Making a pile. A pile. He'll be able to buy me and sell me when he comes back. Mrs Hasson doesn't take it well at all. Isn't she terrified he'll marry a black girl and come back and make a show of us all? Red or white?'

Roger looked at Helen.

'Red.'

'God made us all, I said to her, but she's a hard woman to convince. I had a word with that new young Father Mulcahy about it. Her nerves were getting real bad over the whole thing. Shocking. Wine. I have a few bottles. I always like to keep a few bottles in the place. You never know the moment when someone won't pop in for a meal and ask for a bottle of wine. I have red all right. . . .'

He turned and gazed along the rows of bottles standing on shelves behind the bar.

'What did Father Mulcahy say?' Helen hated a story to be left in mid-air.

'Ah, what would he say? She suffers from the exeema you know. The doctor can't do a thing about it. When her nerves get bad it breaks out all over her.'

'How awful.'

'Spanish there is. Rio ... ja three quid the bottle. Or French. That's more expensive. Four eighty. The French white is cheaper. We'll cross that river when we come to it, Mrs Hasson. That was what Father Mulcahy said. Standing out there in the hall. I mean what more could he say? Just don't be worrying your head about it, he said that to her.'

'What more indeed,' murmured Helen.

'I think we'll have the French red please, Mr Hasson.'

'Right you be, sir.'

He took down a bottle from the shelf, watching himself all the time in the mirror that duplicated the bottles. He watched Roger and Helen watching him. All tidily duplicated. He wiped the dust from the bottle with a cloth and turned it round and placed it on the counter. He reached under the bar for two glasses which he placed neatly beside the bottle.

'Never suffered from exeema?' he asked Helen.

She shook her head.

The cork screw already had a cork impaled on it which he twisted off with his fingers and then threw behind him onto the floor.

'You were spared.'

He belonged to the old school of those who put the bottle between their knees and withdrew the cork with a certain amount of effort. Helen wondered how Roger managed about things like corks.

'Not much call for wine.' The word much puffed out of him as he pulled. 'Take them glasses over to the fire, Mrs Cuffe, and I'll give the gentleman the bottle.' He gave another pull and the cork came away this time. 'There's a bit of smoke from the fire today. It's the wind in the west. Mrs Hasson always wants to instal the electric fires, but there's nothing like the open fire I always think and you don't notice the smoke all that much. There's pleasure in sitting by the open fire.'

Roger followed her over to the fire and put the bottle on the table. He picked up the poker and approached the dismal smoking fire.

'That's right,' called Mr Hasson across the room. 'Give it an old wallop with the poker, a good dunt.'

Roger pushed the poker into the sad heart of the fire and

tried to raise the sods; ash whirled in the air for a moment with the smoke.

'I'm not cold anyway,' said Helen.

'It's the gloom of it,' whispered Roger. 'Would you rather . . .?'

'I'll leave you to your peace.' Mr Hasson retreated from behind the bar back into the hotel again.

'Never mind the gloom, Roger. Let's try the Léoville Barton 1969.' He laughed and put the poker back in the grate. He poured two glasses of wine and sat down beside her.

'Cheers.'

'Cheers.'

The wine was acid.

They grinned almost childishly across the glasses at each other.

'What's fact or fantasy?' he said. 'Madness or sanity? We all live our lives in our own way. It's only when we become confused, disturbed in our own mind about things, that we should start to worry. I am neither confused nor disturbed.'

'I envy your conviction. I've flitted for so long from one half-thought out truth to another, I've had no convictions worth bothering anyone about. I'm not even sure why I started to paint again. It certainly wasn't a desire to say something important to the world.'

There was a long silence. Somewhere outside someone switched on a radio, something country and western plucked and moaned.

'I don't have anything to say anyway . . . that isn't pitifully thin.'

'Perhaps you're not the best judge.'

She ignored him.

'It would be so much easier if I wanted to paint charming landscapes for tourists. You see them all round the place in gift shops. Fifty pounds a crack. Something to remind you of your holiday in dear old Donegal. Blue mountains, thatched cottages, a donkey or two. Efficient. All bloody efficient. Dan tried to persuade me to do that years ago.' She smiled. 'We had quite a row about it. He simply could not understand why I wouldn't do it. We both said quite a lot of silly things to each other.'

Roger rattled his fingers on the table. Rhythmic beats.

'We usually said nothing to each other.'

He stopped drumming for a moment and touched her hand. She didn't seem to notice.

'I think I was a sore disappointment to him. I wonder why nobody ever tells us the truth?'

He was rattling again. The wine in their glasses trembled.

'Truth? My dear girl, if they started to tell us the truth we'd all jump back into the womb again and refuse to come out. . . . Anyway people need those lies to keep themselves going. The more often you repeat something the more likely it is to become true. I was meant for you . . .' he sang the words softly '. . . and you were meant for me. . . .' The fingers beat out the rhythm after his voice had stopped.

'Slow foxtrot,' he said. 'Remember the slow foxtrot?'

'There's one thing.' Her voice was low. He had to lean across the table to catch the words. He kept his fingers quiet. 'For such a long time I've wanted to say this to someone . . . but the right person never seemed to be around. I have never had either a priest or a psychiatrist . . . or perhaps a friend. You know Dan was shot?' She looked across the table towards him. He nodded. 'That in itself was terrible. That brutality. Unforgiveable, really. I found it unforgiveable. I still feel that, each time I read about another . . . snatching of a life . . . I feel that same unforgiveness rising inside me. I don't mean I want vengeance or anything like that. I just feel I'd like the . . . well, perpetrator to know that I will never forgive him. Or her.' She smiled slightly. 'I don't suppose anyone would be too worried by the awfulness of that threat. It's terribly un-Christian though.'

She reached into her pocket and brought out the box of cigarettes. She stood the box on the table in front of her.

'That's not really what I wanted to say. After the shock, the disbelief, the confusion I felt happy. I mean I never mourned his leaving my life, never missed him. I never cried in the night because he wasn't there any more. I felt happy. I haven't dared to say those words to anyone before.' She opened the box and snatched a cigarette and put it in her mouth. She sat there staring at him, with the cigarette dangling from the corner of her lips. He put his hand out again and touched hers. He ran his fingers over the bumps of her knuckles and the wrinkling skin. He traced the blue veins with his finger.

'How do you feel now?' he asked.

She pondered for moment.

'Much the same as I did ten minutes ago.'

'So much for confession.'

He took his hand away from hers and plucked the cigarette out of her mouth and put it back in the box.

'We'll abandon the goat's piss,' he said. 'Lets go to McFaddens in Gortahork and have a real bottle of wine and some food. A night out. Hey?'

'I. . . .' She looked down at her overall. 'I. . . .'

'Yes or no? No rumbling and mumbling about clothes or washing. Yes or . . .?'

She laughed.

'Yes.'

*

It was late, the sky alive with stars and a hard bright moon hanging just out of hand's reach. He stopped the car outside her door. The glass porch glittered and reflected moon and night brightness. She opened the car door and got out. Politely he did the same, or, she wondered, did he have some ulterior motive.

She looked up at the sky.

'What is the stars, Joxer? What is the stars?'

'I had a telescope once. Oh . . . a long time ago. I rather fancied myself as a star gazer when I was about fifteen. I used to spend hours wrapped in a blanket on the roof, searching for something new. A comet or something that no one had ever seen before. Hawthorne's Comet.'

'No luck?'

'No luck.'

'It's been a lovely evening. Thank you.'

She moved round towards the gate.

'I hope you didn't find the drive home too much of a strain.'

'I never worried for a moment. That's drink for you. Had I been sober I would have been in a state of nerves the whole way home. Thank you, Helen.' He held his hand out towards her. She put her hand in his and he bent and kissed it. Then he stood quite formally by the gate as she took the six steps along the little path to the door. She turned the handle. She felt the warmth of the house touch her as the door opened.

'Goodnight,' she said. 'Come and have a meal on Saturday evening . . . and protect me from Jack and his friend.'

'Yes. I'd like that. Goodnight.'

She moved into the porch.

'Helen,' he called.

She turned back towards him. From where she stood she could only see the whole side of his face. Silver sculpture. He looks quite Roman, she thought, a bit grim, like Romans always seemed to look.

'Yes?'

'I've had women you know. I'm not. . . .'

'You don't have to tell me things like that,' she shouted at him. 'I can't bear people who tell me things like that.'

He nodded. He reached into the car and took the keys from the dashboard. He shut the door carefully and walked off along the road towards the station. She watched him as far as the corner, body stiff and slightly stooped. Man in the moon, not a Roman, she thought. She closed the door quietly so as not to disturb his walking silence.

When she got up the next morning and looked out of the window the car had gone.

*

It was a long drive. Boring afternoon, boring dusk, boring darkness across the entire flatness of the country.

Jack remembered as they passed through Boyle that he hadn't telephoned to Helen to say they would be late. She'll be rabid, he thought, and rude.

What the hell?

Boring.

Manus had been asleep since they had left Dublin, or had seemed to be asleep. Not anyway wanting conversation. His head lolled down towards his chest, his hands clasped loosely on his knee as if he were, in fact, at prayer. Even asleep his face looked quite composed, his clothes as well as his face remained uncrumpled. Two pens and the metal-framed glasses tucked into the top pocket of his grey suit gave him the respectable air of a minor official . . . on the way up of course, definitely on the way up.

As they approached Sligo town Jack spoke.

'Will we stop for a drink? I could do with a drink. How about you?'

There was no reply from Manus.

'Manus?'

'Uhhuh?'

One of his hands moved slightly.

'Will we stop for a drink?'

'Where are we?'

He didn't bother to open his eyes.

'Sligo.'

'To hell with Sligo.'

That sounded like no drink.

Jack sighed.

It was a long time before either of them spoke.

'Under bare Ben Bulben's head
In Drumcliffe churchyard Yeats is laid.'

Manus stirred beside him. Raised a hand and rubbed at the side of his nose.

'An ancestor was rector there
Long years ago, a church stands near.
By the road an ancient cross.'

'To hell with Yeats.'

'Cast a cold eye. . . .'

'All poets.'

'On life, on death. Horseman. . . .'

'The Russians have it right.'

'. . . pass by.'

'Prison is the place for poets.'

'That's the only piece of poetry I remember after all those years wasted at school, learning, learning.'

'I don't mean the moon in June types. Let them rant on and on about love and cypress trees and sunsets as long as they like. There's nothing like a good piece of patriotic verse. Workers arise and shake off your chains. Highly commendable. It's when they step out of line. Interfere with the inside of people's heads. Prison.'

'No one reads them. I mean for God's sake, who reads poetry? A few students and a handful of highfalutin' intellectuals.'

'The most insidious form of subversion. The artist's role

should be to enhance, encourage, not undermine. The people must speak with one voice. I believe it is possible to achieve the perfect society. Perhaps the artists may have to be sacrificed.'

'I never know when you're pulling my leg.'

'You have an easy leg to pull. Where are we?'

'Bare Ben Bulben's head is on our right.'

'I may have heard of Yeats, but I never learnt any geography. How much longer dismal driving?'

'You've been asleep.'

'On and off.'

'Why did you never take up driving?'

'I couldn't be bothered. There's always someone around to give you a lift. No point in heaping that sort of hard work on yourself.' He paused for a long time. 'The old eyes aren't great, if you want the truth. No need to spread it round.'

'About an hour,' said Jack. 'A bit more perhaps. My mother may be angry. Don't mind her.'

'No. I don't suppose I will.'

He closed his sore eyes and appeared to sleep again.

'Horseman pass by,' said Jack with resignation.

It was after half past eleven when they arrived in the village. Three street lamps and the odd glow from behind tightly pulled private curtains, no dogs or even drunks were about. As Jack turned the corner and began the uphill drive Manus opened his eyes. His head turned slightly to the left, his eyes glistened for a moment in the light from one of the lamps.

'I can't stand the country. I feel my life falling apart further out of town than the Phoenix Park, for God's sake. Are we nearly there?'

'Two minutes.'

'I hate silence. And darkness. And bloody culchies picking their noses.'

'You're going to have a very painful couple of days.'

'All for Ireland.'

They both laughed for a moment, and then the cottage was there, a light shining in the porch.

'That's it,' said Jack. He pulled over to the side of the road and stopped the car.

Manus got out and stretched his arms above his head,

wriggled his stiff shoulders, took the cottage into his eyes.

'I've always been told that Protestants didn't live in cottages.'

Jack laughed. He opened the back door of the car and took out their bags.

'It just shows how misinformed you've been all these years. Here.' He held Manus's bag out towards him. Manus took it. Jack opened the gate and they walked the few steps to the hall door.

'Breathe that air,' said Jack. 'That's great air.'

'Give me petrol fumes and the smell of the gas works.'

Helen was in the sitting room watching the advertisements on the television.

She was in her dressing gown and bare feet with her hair still damp hanging down around her shoulders. Like as though she was still young, thought Jack. Not fifty, getting on.

She stood up when they came into the room and switched off the set.

'Have you never heard of a telephone?' she said.

'I'm sorry, mother.'

'I was just about to have a last cigarette and go to bed. Waiting . . . waiting is so tiring.' She looked past Jack at Manus. 'Hello.'

'This is Manus.'

'Hello, Manus.'

Manus nodded his head and mumbled something.

She went over to Jack and kissed him.

'You're forgiven. I saw a tangled heap of metal on the road somewhere. I'm like that.'

'All the telephones we tried were vandalised,' lied Jack.

She laughed. 'Don't bother with that rubbish,' she said.

Manus spoke. 'It was my fault, Mrs Cuffe, I held him up leaving Dublin. Slap me if you like.' He held his hand out towards her. She ignored the playful gesture.

'You must be exhausted. Go and put your things in your room and I'll get you both a drink. I've put up the camp bed in your room, Jack, you can both argue about who sleeps where. I've only the two bedrooms,' she explained sideways to Manus.

Another myth shattered, thought Jack.

When they went into the kitchen, ten minutes later, she was stirring something in a saucepan on the stove.

'Help yourselves to a drink. There's just soup and scrambled eggs. I hope that's okay?'

'That's fine.'

Jack poured out two glasses of whisky and shoved the water jug towards Manus.

'You? Mother?'

'No thanks. I'm going to bed quite soon. I'm getting up early to work these days.'

Manus put a drop of water into his whisky and drank the lot in one large gulp. 'God, I needed that.' He looked meaningfully at the bottle. Jack poured him another measure.

'Thanks.' He clasped both hands around the glass as if he were afraid that someone might try to take it from him.

'Are you in college with Jack?' asked Helen.

Manus laughed.

She turned from the scrambled egg to stare at him.

'No,' said Jack.

'I have been educated in the university of life,' said Manus, still laughing.

'Ah.'

She continued with the stirring.

'The Brothers slung me out at fifteen and said never darken our doors again. It was their loss.'

'He's a joker,' said Jack.

'So I gather. Will you have some soup, Manus? Jack, deal with the soup will you?'

'What sort of soup?' asked Manus.

'Well . . . vegetable mainly.'

'No thanks. I only like tomato soup. Heinz.'

'Oh! Do you want some, Jack?'

'Ah . . . no thanks, mother. I'll just have eggs. Just eggs. We'll both just have eggs.'

'Dear me,' she said.

She bent down and took two plates from the oven and scooped scrambled eggs on to both of them.

'There you are. There's toast on the table. I'll leave you to yourselves. Have you plans for tomorrow?'

'Don't worry about us, we'll. . . .'

'Yes,' said Manus. 'We've plans.'

'Roger Hawthorne is coming to supper.'

'Is that the man with the station?' Manus asked.

'Yes.'

'I've always had a great interest in the railways. Isn't that so, Jack?'

'Absolutely.'

'Ebsolutely,' mimicked Manus, somewhat unkindly.

Helen ran water into the scrambled egg saucepan.

'I'm going to bed. Just help yourselves to anything you want.'

'Steam engines were before my time. I never cease to regret that fact. Before your time too, Jack. Isn't that a very regrettable fact?'

'Eat your scrambled eggs and shut up.'

As Helen passed Jack on her way to the door, she put her hand on the top of his head. The corrugated texture of his hair reminded her for a startling moment of Don. She thrust her hand into her pocket and moved to the door. 'If you want me in the morning I'll be in the shed. Otherwise just do whatever you want yourselves. Goodnight.'

Manus bowed politely towards her.

'Goodnight, mother,' said Jack.

*

Jack was awakened the next morning by Manus moving round the room, the electric shaver in his hand, buzzing away at his face. His left hand followed the shaver down the contours of his face feeling for stubble.

'Up, up,' he said as Jack turned over and looked at him. 'No fucking mirror.'

'You seem to be managing very well without one.'

'Up. There's only one way to get out of bed painlessly . . . open the eyes and out. If you stop to think about it at all, you might stay there all day.' He took his finger off the starter and the buzzing stopped. He rubbed at his chin vigorously with his left hand.

'Baby's bottom,' he said. He began to shave the other side of his face. Jack got out of bed and put on his slippers.

'Breakfast,' he said.

'Yeah,' said Manus. 'Let's have a good breakfast. A slap-up feed . . . save us having lunch. Sense?'

'Sense,' agreed Jack and went into the kitchen.

No mother.

Of course no mother.

Jack sighed and opened the fridge. He took out bacon and eggs and tomatoes. Manus came into the room, fully dressed and a slight touch of aftershave.

'Does your man know we're coming?'

'No.'

'I hope we have no trouble with him. There's a cat wanting in the window.'

'Let it in.'

'I get asthma from cats.'

'I've never known you to have asthma.'

'Hay fever, eczema, spots. Let's make it quite clear we won't take any trouble from him.'

Jack was spooning fat over the eggs, watching the yolks turning from yellow to pale pink. The white frilled round the edges.

'What do you mean by trouble?'

'Watch those eggs. I hate mine burnt. Turn down that heat a little.'

'It's a range.'

'Well whatever it is, don't burn my fucking egg.'

Jack moved the pan to the edge of the ring.

'Argument, prevarication, codology of any sort. I like it hard but not turned.'

'Sit down and pour yourself a cup of tea for God's sake, you're making me nervous.'

Manus moved away.

'Mother not cook breakfast?'

'I think she must be across the yard working.'

'Oh yes, you said she painted.'

He pulled out a chair and sat down. The cat stared unblinkingly through the glass at him.

'Any good? Any money in it?'

'I don't know. I've never seen any of her stuff. It's probably awful. She only took it up a couple of years ago. She studied art before she was married. I presume this is some sort of menopausal madness.'

Jack took a quick look at Manus as he said this. Manus always hated that sort of remark. He pursed his lips slightly in disapproval. Jack smiled internally.

'Egg,' said Manus.

Jack scooped one of the eggs off the pan and onto a plate. Two slices of bacon, a tomato cut in quarters and a piece of fried bread. He put the feast down in front of Manus and then took his egg off the pan.

'Do cats really give you all those things, or can I let him in?'

'Let him in if you insist.'

As Jack went over to the window the cat jumped from the sill and walked away across the yard.

'He seems to have some objection to you too,' said Jack. 'I hope your egg's okay.'

'We can manage without him. If he argues at all, that might be best. It'll be best not to tell him too much to begin with. He might not be secure.'

'I doubt that.'

Manus cut himself a slice off the pan.

'He might try to be clever.'

'He wouldn't split. Maybe he won't co-operate, but he wouldn't split.'

'We haven't the right to take chances. You mustn't let your bourgeois liberal attitudes colour your judgments.'

'I don't have bourgeois liberal attitudes.'

Manus laughed and began to wipe the white bread round and round his plate, mopping up all the remaining juices and flavours.

'If you could catch sight of yourself,' he said, shoving the bread into his mouth.

'You'd win an Olympic Gold for speedy eating,' said Jack.

'No point in letting good food get cold on your plate.' He stretched across the table for a piece of toast. 'My mother always said feed the inner man.'

Butter.

'I don't think that's got anything to do with eating,' said Jack.

Marmalade.

'Sure it has. To her at any rate. The inner man is all those coils of intestines, seventeen miles of intestines. Did you know that we have seventeen miles of intestines?'

'No,' said Jack.

'Something like that anyway. That's what she means. It takes a lot of food to keep all that in full working order. A woman is never done cooking, she says . . . feeding the inner man.'

'And woman?' suggested Jack.

'That's good marmalade.' Manus took his first ever bite of Cooper's Oxford. 'Better than Little Chip.'

Jack sighed. He preferred to think of Manus as a leader, a plan-maker, his mind and energy geared towards action, not the eternal talk that went on and on with all the rest. Reminders of his reality always unnerved Jack.

'There's Doherty, Sweeney and Fehily in Dungloe.'

He pushed a corner of toast into his mouth as he spoke.

'And Clancy. Where's Clancy?'

Jack shook his head. It was a rhetorical question. He wasn't supposed to know where Clancy was.

Manus stood up suddenly. His plate was polished clean, his cup was empty, a few scattered crumbs on the table and a drift of tea leaves up the side of his cup were the only evidence that someone had recently eaten.

'We'll go and take a look at her pictures and then we'll have a quick look for your man. We won't waste too much time on him.'

'I . . .' Jack wondered about his mother for a moment.

'Come on,' said Manus impatiently.

They crossed the yard and opened the door of the shed. She was crouched on the floor dragging paint across a canvas with a rag. She was in her dressing gown and her hair was pulled tightly back from her eyes into an elastic band. The room smelt of turpentine and cigarette smoke.

Good heavens, thought Jack, she really does paint.

She seemed to drag her head up and around to look at them as they came in. Her eyes and mind took some time to focus on them.

'Good Lord,' she said. 'I'm sorry. . . .'

Manus interrupted Jack.

'I thought I'd like to see your pictures.' He walked over to where she was crouching. 'He told me you made pictures.'

She put the rag down on the floor and then rubbed her fingers on the front of her dressing gown. She stood up slowly, stiffly. She smiled slightly as she moved and Jack thought for a moment she was going to make some awful joke. She didn't.

'Yes, I make pictures. You're welcome to look at them.'

He frowned down at the canvas on the floor.

'And you too, Jackson . . . you are also welcome.'

Irony in her voice.

'Why do you paint on the floor? I thought . . .?'

Manus made a gesture in the air, indicating an easel.

'I thought I'd better not get an easel before I knew whether I could paint or not. That would have seemed to be tempting providence. Now, I've got used to the floor. Mind you . . . I do get stiff, so perhaps I'll have to get an easel after all. An admission of old age and decrepitude rather than anything else. I'm only starting on that one. Laying down a sort of background.'

'Don't you use a brush?'

'Yes, but you don't have to only use brushes. It depends on the effect you want to get.'

'I see.' His voice was polite but fairly uninterested.

She waved her arm.

'Have a look. Be my guest.' She stooped and picked up the cat who was about to step onto the canvas. 'I'm weeding out the sheep from the goats at the moment. I'm trying to put together enough paintings to bring up to Dublin. I hope perhaps that someone will take me on. Let me show you some of these little water colours. I need a framer badly. I thought that maybe . . .' she stopped abruptly and spread four of the water colours out on the table . . . 'I think I'll have to bring them to Dublin to be framed. It costs a lot you know to get a picture ready for sale.'

Manus nodded.

For a short while none of them moved. The cat rubbed his head against her shoulder.

Jack was staring at the man on the beach. The shadow lay long on the furrowed sand. God, he thought, it was right what I said to Manus . . . menopausal madness. Sad to think of your fifty-year-old mother fantasising about naked young men. The sun hung white and very cold above the young man's head. A searchlight, he thought.

'They're nice so they are,' said Manus.

'I'm working more with oil at the moment.'

Jack moved away from the painting, over to look at the watercolours on the table. Nicely painted, he had to give her that. Sheep, trees, safe pastoral subjects. I must ask her for a couple for my rooms in College, he thought, and then looked across the room once more at the man on the beach. For a moment it became Damian Sweeney. The shock of that gripped him inside his body. He felt himself blushing and turned quickly away. Jesus, he thought. Jesus. He looked again and saw only a lank figure, feet in a wisp of sea, black shadow marks.

'We should be off,' he said.

'I'm working on a series.' She pointed towards the painting. '"Man on a Beach."' She giggled. 'Not what you might call a very original title. I'm working on number two at the moment.'

Manus stared in silence at the painting.

'Who's the fella?' he asked at last.

'No one in particular. Purely a figment.'

'Not Jack?'

She burst out laughing.

'Not Jack. I haven't seen Jack naked since he was about ten and I used to rush into the bathroom and scrub his filthy neck from time to time. He has always been the very essence of modesty . . . at least as far as I am concerned.'

Manus smiled.

'The very essence of modesty,' he repeated. 'I like that. That's good.'

'We should be getting on.'

'Now, who would buy a thing like that?' Manus nodded his head towards the painting.

'Perhaps nobody,' she answered.

'And yet you paint it . . . on spec so to speak.'

'Yes.'

'Would you say it was art?'

'That's really for someone else to say, not me.'

He nodded.

'Manus . . .' said Jack. 'We should be getting on.'

'Right you be. He's going to show me a bit of the countryside, Mrs Cuffe.'

'If you're not back by half past eight we'll eat without you, and I'll be raging, Jack, really raging.'

'Don't fuss,' said Jack.

*

'No,' said Mrs Sweeney. She'd no idea at all where Damian was. Hadn't seen neither hide nor hair of him for the last two days. Never said a word nor left a message.

'No,' she said. How could you tell when he'd be back if he hadn't even said he was going? It could be Galway. There was an uncle in Galway he visited from time to time. Didn't he work for the Englishman above at the station and wouldn't he likely be back on Monday morning?

'Yes.' She'd say they'd called looking for him. That would be the sum total of the help she'd be able to give them.

Two red-haired childred stood by her side, nodding as she spoke.

A silent dog ran beside the car for the best part of half a mile as Jack drove away.

Neither of them spoke.

In the few weeks Jack had been away the leaves had been blown from the hedges. Thorns and fuchsias were now bare. The first gap in the hedge was the track through the caravan park and up onto the dunes above the beach. Jack turned through it and they bumped across the grass and up the hill until they could go no further. Below them stretched the wide beach and the sea.

'Is this where your mother paints naked fellas?' Manus' voice was sour.

Jack didn't say a word.

Manus pulled a bar of Fruit and Nut from his pocket and unwrapped it. He opened the window a crack and let the blue and silver papers scatter away with the wind. He then proceeded to eat the chocolate.

'Fucking culchies.'

He stared in hatred at the sea as he chewed.

'I wouldn't stand there with my feet in the sea and let any woman paint me.'

'She said it was a figment of her imagination.'

Manus laughed.

'Figment my backside. Fig leaf.' He laughed again at his own joke. 'Fig leaf.'

He took a handkerchief from the pocket and wiped the chocolate from his fingers.

'I've said it again and again and you're my witness, there's no use expecting anything from the fools around the country. Fucking slíbhíns. Full of hot air. Words, talk, but try to get them to do anything and they disappear to Galway or down a rabbit hole. Doherty, Sweeney, Fehily.' He shook his head. 'We'll not engage anyone further in this. It's only a staging post we need. You know the lay of the land.'

'Yes,' said Jack.

Below them the wind caught the top layer of the sand and blew it along the length of the beach. Jack remembered how his bare legs used to sting as the grey and golden grit was blown against them.

'We'll take a look at this railway shed that you were talking about. That shouldn't be any problem. This guy . . . the owner . . . sounds like a bit of a nutter.'

'A war hero,' said Jack, his eyes still on the racing sand. 'Blown apart in World War Two and then sewn together again.'

Manus smiled slightly.

'I can't get over the thought of that fella standing down there and letting your mother draw pictures of him in his skin. Ballybofey.'

Jack turned on the engine.

'War hero.' Manus smiled again. 'I have a man to see in Ballybofey. You can have a drink or go for a walk.'

He was like that. Never let his right hand know what his left hand was up to. Jack backed away from the edge of the dune and then turned carefully in the caravan park. On a line at the back of one of the vans a forgotten dish cloth flapped forlornly in the wind. They bumped over the grass and out onto the road.

'Ballybofey,' said Manus.

Jack turned left. Manus leant forward and pressed the button of the radio. They drove, each one thinking his own thoughts, Radio Two pulping past their ears.

*

For some reason Helen had taken the six candlesticks out of the kitchen cupboard and unwrapped them from the yellow dusters in which they had lain comfortably for so long. She had even cleaned them and hated the way the skin on her fingers had stiffened and smelt with the ingrained pink polish. Handsome Georgian silver, not too many curlicues. Might get a few bob for them one day if the need ever arose. Candles are nice, she thought. People look so gold and secret. All faces divide quite in half, black shadows make caves and the gold is soft, malleable. Faces look medieval; that is too romantic a thought. Jack's friend has eyes like sharp bright stones.

'What are you thinking? You've disappeared from us.'

Roger's voice.

She turned to him.

'I'm sorry. I was just thinking how beautiful we all look by candlelight. Our warts are eliminated.'

He looked around the table.

'I wouldn't say they were eliminated, made mysterious perhaps. You and I . . . our . . . I won't say old . . . our used, experienced faces are mysteriously beautiful. . . . The two young men with smooth untouched faces merely look boring.'

'I object,' said Jack.

'Objection overruled,' Helen laughed. 'For once let the young be at a disadvantage.'

'Don't you find your mother mysterious?' asked Roger.

'No.'

'Oh dear. I always found my mother mysterious. Perhaps that was because she was killed before I was old enough to have looked at her realistically. And you. . . .'

He turned to Manus, who was twiddling his glass round and round in his fingers. Candle flames danced in the wine. 'Do you have a mother?'

'Of course I have a mother . . . just a straightforward run-of-the-mill mother. No mysteries.' He looked across the table at Helen almost accusingly.

'I don't believe in mysteries. There are conjuring tricks, but no magic, as far as I'm concerned.'

'Ghosts?' asked Helen.

'In people's heads. Too many bloody ghosts in people's heads.'

'Don't you find it boring to have an explanation for everything?'

'On the contrary, I have never felt bored in my life. Boredom is quite a disease of the middle classes you know. I know what I'm doing and why I get on and do it.'

'May we ask?' Roger pulled at his eye patch for a moment as he spoke.

'Ask what you like. I don't have to answer any questions that I don't want to. This isn't Castlereagh.'

Helen balanced her cigarette on its end on her plate and watched the smoke rise thin and straight into the darkness above them.

'I hate cross-examinations,' she said. 'I think there are so many things inside each of us that we don't want to say, and that other people don't want to hear. We could become quite unfriendly. . . .' Her voice trailed away like the smoke.

'How do you mean, mother?'

'Well . . . political perhaps . . . I'd rather not . . . be forced to make judgments.'

Jack laughed sharply.

'One day, mother, your ivory tower will fall down. Then where will you be? Then you'll have to ask questions . . . answer questions . . . draw conclusions.'

'If my ivory tower, as you call it, falls down, I'll build another one.' She got up and began to move the plates from the table. 'And I'll always prefer my mysteries to your conclusions. There's chocolate mousse. Who wants some chocolate mousse?'

They all wanted chocolate mousse.

She took it out of the fridge and put it in the middle of the table. That was for Jack anyway, she thought, as she handed each of them a plate. Chocolate mousse for Jack.

'And miracles.' She sat down again. 'Help yourselves.' She picked up the smoking cigarette and crushed it out onto the plate. 'I believe in miracles. Not the bleeding heart kind.'

'What would you consider to be a miracle, Mrs Cuffe?' Manus' voice was curious.

'Well . . . I suppose the intervention of something quite outside your own experience into your. . . . Something perhaps that permits a revelation of yourself. I think the intervention permits the miracle rather than is the miracle itself. I seem to gather thoughts, ideas in my head that I can't express in coherent words. Perhaps that's why I paint. I have to expose some truth.'

She muttered the last words to herself.

'Give us an example,' said Jack. 'Tell us about one of your own private and personal miracles.'

She shook her head.

'One thing is clear to me . . .' Roger broke into the silence . . . 'this chocolate mousse is a miracle. That's for certain sure.'

She laughed.

'No, no, no. It's the only thing I can cook with complete conviction that it is going to turn out all right. Correct, Jack?'

'Pretty well correct. Even Gran. . . .'

'Your grandmother couldn't make a chocolate mousse like mine if she lit a million candles to the patron saint of cooks or crawled seven times round the Black Church on her hands and knees. It was my single personal triumph over your grandmother.'

'Helen tells me that you are interested in trains.'

'That's right. My granda was a fireman in the old GNR. He has never done telling us stories. He made you believe that nothing in the world was ever like the Dublin Belfast run.'

Jack looked towards him with admiration.

'Steam. Of course I don't remember the steam myself . . . only his stories.'

'No,' said Roger. 'You wouldn't remember the steam. That would have been before your time.'

'Every Sunday afternoon until just before he died he'd step off to the marshalling yards beyond Amiens Street . . . that's what he always called it . . . Amiens Street. He and several other old guys, have a bit of a rabbit about the way things used to be. It's funny the way old people always think that things are worse now instead of better. He used to rave about things when he got home, carelessness, dirt, incompetence.'

Perhaps he's talking the truth, thought Jack. I know so little about him.

'I used to go with him sometimes. There was a lot of old stock in the sheds there never saw the light of day. I enjoyed it when I was a kid. But then . . . well you've heard all the old stories a thousand times, and you find you've better things to do than listening to old footplatemen trying to pretend they haven't one foot in the grave.'

'I'd be delighted to show you the station. Delighted. When can you come over?'

'Tomorrow. We'll be free all day until the evening. We have to set off back then. That's right isn't it, Jack ... we could manage tomorrow morning?'

'Splendid. I'll expect you then ... about ten thirty. Helen, will you come with them?'

She shook her head.

'I think not, thank you. Have some more chocolate mousse.'

*

'I must say, you've done a great job. I'd like the granda to have seen that box. He wasn't into this narrow gauge stuff being a city man, but he'd have really appreciated that box.'

'Thank you,' said Roger. He looked as if he hadn't slept all night. His eye was fretful, his face pale and without much life.

'What are you working on at the moment?'

'The crossing gates. Damian is replacing a lot of the timbers. They were badly rotted. That shouldn't take too long. They'll have to remain manual for a while, but we hope to automate them before too long. It's a nuisance that, in bad weather, but it can't be helped.'

'How about the track?'

Manus walked along the edge of the platform and looked down at the weeds.

'We'll clear that. All that mess will die back when the winter comes. Until I see the state of the track I can't say how long that will take. I may have to call in some outside help if we need to re-lay any sleepers.'

'What's that shed over there?'

'I think this was mainly a goods stop. Stuff must have been stored there for local farmers to come and collect. I have been surprised myself at its size. I don't use it. It's quite a decent piece of railway architecture though, I'd hate to pull it down. No doubt we'll find a use for it some day.'

'No doubt. Mind if I go and have a look?'

'By all means. Excuse me if I don't come with you. Sometimes I feel quite unwell.'

'Is there anything we can do?' asked Jack. 'I could run over to the doctor for you.'

'No. I just like to be left alone. There isn't anything anyone can do. . . .' He turned away from them and walked towards the house slowly. At the door he stopped. 'Go ahead,' he said. 'It's not locked . . . just the bolt.'

Without even saying goodbye he went into the house.

They walked in silence to the end of the platform and then across the tracks. The shed had a wooden door in surprisingly good condition, held closed by a large iron bolt. It had been oiled at some stage and slid back without fuss. Inside, dust, cobwebs and dead flies veiling the small windows and a large empty space.

'It's one of your mother's miracles,' said Manus.

Jack pushed the door shut behind them and looked around. 'I think it's a crazy idea.'

'Why?' Manus' voice was shrill. 'What's crazy about it? They don't use it . . . don't touch it. There's no one else for miles around. No nosey kids even.'

'You wouldn't know what he'd do, for God's sake . . . or Damian. How will you get the stuff in and out of here without him finding out?'

'Leave it to me, why don't you? You just do what you're told. Have I ever let anyone down? Answer me that. Have I bungled? Hey? Have I?'

'No. But. . . .'

'But fucking nothing.'

'I think you're as mad as he is.'

Manus ignored that. He stared around the shed, his eyes glittering with excitement. He put his hand into his coat pocket and pulled out a bar of chocolate. He unwrapped it and shoved the paper back into his pocket.

'The trouble is,' he began to munch at the bar, 'with people like yourself, you've no imagination.'

'As far as the set-up is concerned, I've too much imagination.'

'Always picking. I don't know why I'm lumbered with you.'

'You know well why you're lumbered with me . . . you sent me down to talk to Damian. You needed to use my car. That's why. You have a marginal, menial use for me.'

'That's right. Now that you have it clear in your mind can we drop the subject?'

He finished the chocolate in silence.

'I simply feel,' said Jack, 'that I could be used in some more constructive way. I am, after all. . . .'

'You're not an active service guy.'

'I. . . .'

'You're not. You can take it from me. You are most usefully employed in helping to produce a back-up service.'

'I. . . .'

'People like you faint at the sight of blood.'

'You haven't the faintest idea whether I faint at the sight of blood or not. You've never given me the chance to find out.'

'I know what I'm talking about. If you want to stay with us . . . be useful . . . very useful. For God's sake what do you want . . . the whole organisation to fall apart without you? Be your age. If you want to be useful then do what you're told. Okay.'

Jack nodded,

'We'll win you know. Then you'll probably be quite glad I didn't allow you to get up to anything. . . . You can never tell when the bourgeois conscience will begin to prick. There aren't really too many of us who have the clear eye.' He laughed. 'And a steady hand.'

He took out his handkerchief and wiped the chocolate from round his mouth.

'I need you.'

He folded the handkerchief so that the chocolate stains were inside and then put it back in his pocket.

'You need the clear eye. Only the vision counts. Some people find that hard to take.'

'I suppose you're right.'

'That's the ticket. Come on . . . we've seen all there is to see here. We'll get back to Dublin as soon as possible after lunch.'

He opened the door and they went out into the sunshine.

'I presume your mother'll be giving us lunch?'

'I imagine so, yes.'

They crossed the line and went out into the road through a little wicket gate by the level crossing and walked round to the front of the station where the car was waiting.

'I'd say she had a clear eye,' said Manus.

'Who?'

'Your old lady.'

Jack laughed.

'Tell me,' he asked as they got into the car. 'Was your grandfather really a railwayman?'

'Sure thing. He'd have loved that station. A really great job that Englishman has done.'

'And Damian.'

Jack started the engine.

'Bugger Damian.'

*

On Wednesday at about half past eleven Damian opened the door without knocking and walked into the kitchen. Mrs O'Sullivan was washing cloths at the sink.

'Look what the cat brought in.'

She wrung black water out of a duster.

'That floor is clean.'

He shuffled his feet on the mat.

'Have you lost your tongue?'

She pulled out the plug and the dirty foamy water circled out through the hole.

'I'm just surprised to find you here, that's all.'

'It just shows how little you know about what goes on. I've been keeping this place in order for the past five year. If you're coming in, come in and close that door behind you.'

He pushed the door shut, remembering as he did so that he'd said he would take a piece off the bottom of it.

She turned on the hot tap.

'Well?'

'Is she about?'

'Who's she? The cat's granny.'

'Mrs Cuffe.'

She threw the cloths into the basin again and agitated them around.

'What do you want with her? She's working.'

'I have a message.'

'She doesn't like to be disturbed when she's working.'

She wrung the duster out again and then cracked it in the air above the basin. His mother went through the same rigmarole, he thought.

'It's a private message.'

She walked across the kitchen to the Aga and hung the cloth on the metal rail above the ovens.

'Is your mother keeping well?'

'She's grand, thanks.'

'I've tea made.' She picked the teapot from the top of the Aga. 'You can take her over a cup and save me the walk across the yard. That's a wind would kill you.'

She took down three mugs from the dresser and carefully filled them with tea, and a few drops of milk, pursing her lips as she poured, disapproving of Damian's presence.

'And yourself.' She nodded towards the mugs. 'Sugar?'

He shook his head.

'Away on. You and your message.'

Helen was startled and pleased by Damian's appearance. She got up from the floor and took the mug of tea from his hand.

'Thanks. What a nice surprise. Sit down. When did you get back?'

There was only one chair and that had a canvas standing on it.

'Or rather I should ask . . . where have you been?' She lifted the picture from the chair and stood it against the wall. 'You did a disappearing act.'

'Is that me?'

He put his mug on the table and moved over the floor towards the painting of the man on the beach.

'Well . . . yes and no.'

He peered closely at the picture, straining his eyes to recognise himself.

'I'm not that thin. Am I?'

'If it looked like you it would be a portrait. It's just a man on a beach. Any man on any beach.'

'I was happy that morning.'

She smiled.

'It was funny being naked in the daytime.'

'Yes,' she said.

'You haven't made it a very happy picture.'

She didn't say anything.

'Why?' He asked after a long silence.

'I just do what I'm told.'

He looked at her.

'I paint. My hands mix and paint and scrub and scrape and squeeze the tubes empty. Light the cigarettes. I move. Down there on the floor.' She pointed to the canvas on the floor. He moved over towards it and stared down at it. A man ran through the unfolding water, light exploded above and behind him in the sky and his huge shadow filled the foreground of the canvas.

'Is that me too?'

'Yes and no.'

'What do you mean you do what you're told?'

He crouched down beside the picture in the position she used for painting.

'There is a voice . . . quite a clear voice. It's always been there, but when I was young it frightened me, so I didn't listen and it went away. If I kept quite still, moved with extreme caution it didn't bother me. I just have to thank God I didn't kill it with my inattention.'

'He hears voices too. I hear him sometimes quarrelling, raging against them.'

'Ghosts,' she said. 'He lives with ghosts.'

Damian stood up. Helen noticed with a certain satisfaction that his knees also cracked.

'Will someone buy them?'

'I hope so.'

'How . . . I mean . . . how?'

'I'm not really too sure what I'll do. But, I think . . . when I've finished this series . . . I have four in my mind . . . then I'll pack them up somehow and a selection of the others and take them up to Dublin. See if I can find a gallery to exhibit them. It probably isn't just as easy as that. I haven't worked that end of things out yet. I will. When this is finished then I'll have time to think about that sort of thing.'

'They're big for packing.'

'Umm.'

'I could maybe make you a box . . . a sort of case out of timber. We've lots of timber above. . . . If only his trains were running, we'd have no transport problem. We can work something out between us.'

'You're very kind.'

'You wouldn't want them damaged. It might have to be padded inside. I'll start thinking up something for you.' He looked at the two canvases, measuring, judging with his eyes. 'Easy as winking,' he said.

She handed him his mug of tea.

'Drink this up before it gets cold. It'll be some time yet before I'm ready to pack them.'

'I can be sorting out the wood I need . . . and the others, the smaller ones, if I can get to measure them up, I can make another box for them too.'

'Where were you?' she asked.

He took a drink from the mug.

'Why did you go away like that without telling anyone?'

'I just felt like a trip to Galway. I take a run down there from time to time.'

He took another drink.

'About once every couple of months or so. I have cousins, uncles, aunts. My mother's people are from down there. Don't tell me you were worrying after me?'

She looked around for her cigarettes. He saw the box before she did and bent to pick it off the floor.

'Thank you.'

She didn't open the box, just held it in her hand.

'I just wondered if it was anything to do with Jack, that's all. I know it's none of my business.'

'Jack's your business.'

'Not really. Not any longer.'

He drank again, looking straight into her face over the edge of the mug.

'What gives you that idea anyway?'

'Oh . . . I don't know . . . you were angry last week. . . .'

'Oh, that.' He remembered.

She took a cigarette from the box and put it in her mouth. She dropped the box onto the floor.

'I don't like Manus.' He put his hand into his pocket and miraculously took out a box of matches.

'I wasn't mad about him either,' she said.

He put the mug on the table and struck a match. He held it out towards her. She leaned forward and lit the cigarette.

'Thanks. Where did you meet him?'

'Around.' He smiled slightly. 'I'm twenty-four you know, I've been around. Next question?'

'People say things about you.'

'Aye. People say things about anyone who doesn't quite toe the line. That's not a question.'

'I just wondered if they were true.'

'I thought we were talking about Jack.'

'We are. You know as well as I do what I'm talking about. You know right well the question I'm trying to ask.'

He turned away from her and walked over to the window. A huge front of cloud was building up on the horizon.

'The wind is getting up,' he said. 'Helen,' he felt quite brave as he spoke her name. 'Ask me the question. What are you afraid of?'

'Are you in the Provos?'

'No.' He laughed. 'You asked the wrong question.'

'I hate being messed about, confused. I've screwed myself up to hear some sort of truth, I wish you'd get on and tell it to me.'

'What's truth? Manus' truth and my truth wouldn't come within a mile of each other. Perhaps I'll have a cigarette after all.' He held his hand out towards her.

'No. If you've stopped, you've stopped.' But she picked the box off the floor and threw it across the room to him just the same.

'At eighteen, seventeen, sixteen, whenever it is you stop thinking like a child, well to put it a bit differently, start to be your own man. Right?'

She nodded.

'I thought . . . well there has to be more to the whole damn thing than just kick the Brits out and then wham . . . paradise. I thought a bit about how I felt people should be able to live. I talked around a bit. Listened. Read the papers. You've a lot of time to pass when you don't have a regular job. I did odd jobs, here and there. I've never wanted to be a layabout. But I'd time to spare. I joined the Sticks . . . you know . . .?'

'Yes. The Official I.R. . . .'

• He held his hand up.

'Not a word. Excuse me, missus, the Workers' Party. We've gone straight, political. Fight elections, members in Dail Eireann. You must know. . . .'

He pointed the cigarette at her, like an accusing finger.

'I read the papers.'

'I used to run messages for them. Do odd jobs. . . .'

'Quite the little odd-job man you seem to be.' Her voice was angry.

'That was before they . . . modernised . . . saw things in a new light. Shut down . . . that side of things. That was a democratic decision, but. . . .'

'There's always a but, isn't there?'

'There's always a few who like to do things their own way. I did the. . . .'

'Odd jobs again?'

'Aye. A few. Not for a while though I haven't. Not for . . . I lost the heart for that sort of thing.' He laughed suddenly. 'Must be growing old. I don't see much point in killing people. Maybe I'm just wet.'

He put the cigarette in his mouth and then took it out and held it out towards her. 'I thought I was a great guy once upon a time. A God save Ireland hero.' He moved slowly towards her, the cigarette in his outstretched hand. She took it from him and dropped it on the floor.

'You asked the question,' he said after a long silence. He let his hand fall slowly to his side.

'And Manus?'

'Manus doesn't believe in democracy. Manus likes to run things his way. He still believes that the gun is mightier than the word.'

'Why doesn't he join the Provos then?'

Damian laughed.

'The Provos have a structure, an army, rules. They wouldn't look at Manus, only to shoot him.'

She walked over to the chair and sat down. Her shoulders were very stiff.

She needed a spell in a deep hot bath. She needed . . . she needed. . . .

'Jack?'

What the hell about Jack, she thought. Jackson Cuffe. What the hell about him?

'I shouldn't worry too much about Jack. He'll be okay.'

'What do you mean don't worry? Don't be damn silly. He's my son. He's . . . he's. . . .'

He thought she was going to cry. Don't let her cry. He crossed his fingers for luck as he used to do as a child.

'Jack's only in on the edge of this. I mean I think he quite admires Manus ... that sort of thing. I'm not saying his political motives aren't quite pure. I'm sure they are. He's just running messages too, like I was. You don't have to worry. He won't get any further than that. It's quite exciting you know. You feel alive, relevant. Manus knows that. Manus is no dozer.'

She shook her head.

'Well, it is. But Jack hasn't the balls to use a gun. I don't think he could even light a fuse. Like me. I like to think I backed my way out of all that because I thought about it and came to conclusions, but I think I probably didn't have any balls either.'

She lifted her hand and rubbed at the left side of her neck.

'What should I do?' she asked.

'Nothing. Leave him alone. Paint your pictures.'

He put a hand on her shoulder.

'Now you know why I went to Galway. It seemed the easiest thing to do.'

'What did they want you for?'

He shrugged.

'No idea.'

'And you wouldn't tell me if you had.'

'That's right.'

She gave a sudden little burst of laughter.

'Oh God, if his grandmother knew. That bitchy thought makes me feel a little better. Will we go and have a drink?'

'Another time. I must get back. I've stayed too long as it is. I just came around to tell you that he's bad the last couple of days.'

'Bad?'

'He just sits there. I mean it's happened before, but I thought that perhaps you. . . . He likes you. He just sits there. I hate to see him like that.'

'All right, Damian. I'll go over this evening. I'll bring some food . . . supper. . . . If you think. . . .'

'I'd be pleased if you'd do that.'

He moved towards the door.

'I'm sorry.'

'That's all right. I'm glad you told me.'

He nodded and opened the door. As he stepped out into the windy morning she said after him:

'Don't stay away, Damian. We can be friends now.'

He shut the door and went across the yard and out of the gate onto the road. It wasn't until she heard the gate click that she allowed the tears to slide from her eyes.

*

The wind blew up. By four o'clock in the afternoon it was tearing in from the north-west, ripping branches from the startled trees and scattering the remaining leaves from the hedges. The waves frothed like egg whites on the dull surface of the sea. More and more clouds piled up behind the horizon. Gulls, seemingly blown backwards, looked spectral against the grey sky. Everything was grey: the fields, the frenzied trees, the hedges, the distant roofs. Only the birds and the waves startled the eye.

Helen's storm had subsided. By four o'clock in the afternoon the house was filled with the safe smells of cooking and steamy bath water and she sat on the floor in front of the sitting-room fire drying the tangled wet hair that lay stretched across her shoulders. The cat, who always took a personal exception to high winds, was curled, eyes shut, but not asleep, on an armchair.

'Why?' she said directly to the cat. Her hair steamed.

'Wise cat. Answer no silly questions.'

The cat's ears flicked away her words.

Do I have to have a role in this, she wondered? Can't I just paint? Unravel my own mysteries?

She shook her head ferociously and drops of water sizzled into the fire.

If the poor little nameless girl had lived would things have been different? Would I have in some way been forced to face my responsibilities?

Useless now to speculate.

All he learnt from watching me was an obvious distaste for non-involvement. Perhaps that's a mark in his favour.

I thought he loved his father. I relied in a way on that mutual love to keep me guiltless.

What is the point in hashing and re-hashing tired thoughts?

No point.

Perhaps Jack really cares? That too would be a point in his favour. I doubt it somehow. There is so little caring.

A cigarette.
My death defying gesture.
And live a coward
A craven coward.
The tune rocked into her mind.
And live a cow . . . and all my days.
God damn you, Jack, for throwing this rock into the pool of my isolation.

*

It was just dark when she set out to walk to the station, an old-fashioned basket, into which she had tucked a hot pie and fat baked potatoes, over her arm. She was afraid that the wind might blow her and her bicycle into the ditch. She was wearing a long woollen skirt which the wind slammed back against her legs and then pulled and plucked it behind her and her hair and her coat that she held right across her breast with one clutching hand. I'm quite mad to be doing this, she thought as she closed the gate behind her so that the wind wouldn't blow it off its hinges. The cat sat in the window and watched her go, exasperated by her foolishness. He might just send me home again. Might rant, rage at her presumption, or just sit silently until she left again, defeated.

Even from here she could hear the roar of the sea as it crashed on the beach and was sucked out again dragging sand, stones, wrack, only to hurl them once again onto the shore. She thought she should join in the noise with a song, but found that with the strength of the wind in her face she was unable to open her mouth. So she sang in her head instead. Oh Thou that tellest good tidings to Zion, good striding music. She imagined herself blessed with a rich contralto voice. Oh Thou that tellest good tidings to Zion didleiddleiddle did le diddle, Get thee up into the high mountain, from which you would be blown away into outer space this moment, Oh thou that tellest good tidings to Jerusalem diddleidleiddle Arise, shine, for thy Light is come. Handel's walking in the wind music. Arise. Shine. . . . There was no sign of light in the station house as she turned the corner and she thought rather crossly of being pushed and twirled back down the road by the wind. Undignified it would be. The cat would laugh to see her reappear, a pile of refuse in the power of the north westerly. As she approached the house she saw the flicker of firelight from the window of the sitting room. She pushed open the station door and went across the hallway. At the door to the room she paused for a moment, suddenly realising how wild she must look, but she turned the handle and opened the door. He was sitting in a deep chair by the fire. He wasn't asleep, she could see the firelight flicker in his eye.

'May I turn on the light?' she asked.

'Who?' His voice was a murmur.

'Helen.'

She reached out her hand and groped along the wall for the light switch.

They both blinked in the sudden glare.

'Helen.' He pushed himself up out of the chair. 'My dear Helen. I thought you were a ghost. Do come in.'

'It's a night for ghosts. I do hope you don't mind me intruding on you like this.' She closed the door firmly behind her and then walked over and put the basket down on the table. 'I didn't feel like eating alone so I brought some food over here for both of us. Is that all right?'

'I'm not very good company.'

'Neither am I. We can be gloomy together.'

They stood looking at each other in silence for a long time. Then he laughed.

'You are the most wind blown thing I've ever seen. Here, come over to the fire. I'll just put some more wood on it. Let me take your coat.' He stood quite still, unable to think what to do first. She picked the basket up from the table and headed for the kitchen door.

'Before I do anything else, I'm going to put these things in the oven. I'll be right back.' She left him to recover his equilibrium.

By the time she came back he had combed his hair, put on his tweed jacket and done something miraculous to the fire. The overhead light had been switched off and two lamps lit instead. The room looked mellow.

'Metamorphosis,' she said as she looked around.

'It's more welcoming. I'm sorry I was a bit dazed when you arrived. I have whisky or wine. Which would you like?'

'Oh . . . I. . . .'

'Whisky first anyway. Sit down.'

She sat down by the fire and watched him move around the

room. He was amazingly deft, she thought, neat controlled movements, no fumbling.

'I've been a bit off colour these last couple of days, so things are in a bit of a mess. I haven't been keeping things up to the mark. Here.' He handed her a glass of whisky. 'It's good that. Scottish malt. Doesn't need water. Unless you . . .?'

She shook her head.

She sipped. Smokey, potent.

'It's lovely. . . .'

'I suppose Damian told you I wasn't well. Ran around and laid that burden on you.'

She felt her face go red.

'I. . . .'

'He fusses like an old hen. I just get days of . . . I don't know what you'd call it . . . melancholy perhaps. Depression is what they call it now, I think. I prefer the word melancholy. It has a poetic ring about it.' He sat down and raised his glass towards her.

'Sláinte.'

'Sláinte. Life is butter melon cauliflower,' she said and giggled.

'Butter melon, butter melon,' he sang, to her surprise.

'Melon cauliflower.' She joined in.

'Cauliflower.' Neither of them would have won a prize for singing.

'Why didn't you stay in England and become a managing director or a barrister or something like that?'

'Because I'm mad. Haven't I explained that to you before? I am poor mad Roger. I didn't want to be a managing director. I didn't even want to be a chairman. I didn't want anything that they expected me to want. I have been under constraint you know . . . in the nicest possible private homes. Shadowed night and day. Just in case I did myself some harm . . . I don't think even they thought I would harm anyone else. Just myself.'

'Did you . . . would you . . .?'

'I don't think so . . . not even then. Now . . . to spite them I'd like to live to be a hundred. A pauper of a hundred. All that money gone, dissipated. I'd like them to have to pay for my funeral.' He grinned at her. 'You see, melancholy is followed by spleen. Soon, I will be normal again.'

'Do they know where you are?'

He shrugged.

'Probably. I imagine they'll leave me alone for a while though, unless I provoke them in some way. I have no desire to do that at the moment. Have another drink?'

'Are we going to get drunk?'

He got up and came over and took the glass from her hand.

'No. Perhaps we are going to be happy.' He poured some more whisky into both their glasses. 'I'm hungry. Do you know I haven't really eaten since Sunday. Just picked. Poor Damian tried to tempt me with food, but he got eaten instead. I will apologise to him tomorrow.'

'What did you think of Jack's friend?'

He grimaced. He put the glass into her hand and went and got his own.

'Not much. It's hard to tell just like that. Not much. Why?'

'I just wondered.'

'He knows quite a bit about the railways. That was quite nice. Not too many people have that enthusiasm any longer.'

'I suppose not. He's . . . Damian says . . . he's mixed up in . . . involved . . . in violent activity of some sort.'

'Well?'

'And Jack.'

'Ah, yes. Jack.'

His face was quite non-committal.

The fire crackled and she suddenly was reminded of the evening she had been writing the Christmas cards. The fire at her back had crackled.

Fires in the streets.

'You're upset? You're surprised?'

'Yes. Yes, of course. Wouldn't you be?'

'No. At the same age, in the same situation I might well have done the same thing.' He laughed. 'How foolish of me . . . I did . . . only I had no choice. Come come, Helen. Suppose it was the thirties and Jack had gone off to fight in the International Brigade. You'd have felt frightened for him, but a little bit proud. Wouldn't you?'

'I don't know. Sitting here with things the way they are I can't put myself in that position. There has to be some other way.'

He was silent. The fire glowed in his eye.

She thought quite irrelevantly of the Wandering Aengus.

A fire was in my head
I went out to the hazel wood
Because . . .

'Very few people have ever had the courage or the love or the commitment to lead the other way,' he smiled. 'Only two spring to my uneducated mind. Jesus Christ and Gandhi. Look where it got them. Others have talked, preached, moved, yes a bit they've moved but they've been crushed. Viciously crushed. The crushers are always ready. Only in art, Helen, is there any approach to perfection achieved. In living there is none. There never can be. I sometimes think the man with the gun sees things more clearly than we, poor tired creatures of good will.'

'If things had been different . . . .'

'You feel if you had filled him full of moral outrage, picked and plucked at his mind all through his growing years? Rubbish, Helen, rid yourself of that sort of guilt. For God's sake he might have become a chartered accountant.'

They both burst out laughing.

'Finish up your drink,' he said. 'We must go and eat whatever delicacy you have out there in the oven for us. What is it, by the way, so that I can open an appropriate bottle of wine?'

He held out his hand towards her and pulled her gently to her feet.

'A raised chicken pie.'

'My dear Helen, how scrumptious. I haven't had a raised pie since I was a boy. Come along, come along. Happiness is just around the corner.'

*

They asked me how I knew
My true love was true.
I, of course, replied,
Something here inside
Cannot be denied.
Sweet tenor voice turned and turned.
They said some day you'll find
All who love are blind.
When you heart's on fire
You must realise

Smoke gets in your eyes.

They moved together in the middle of the room.

Walking shoes, she thought, are not quite the thing. I should have brought my dancing shoes, like children's parties, over my arm in a cotton bag.

'Will we play the remembering game?' he asked close to her ear.

'No.'

His arm held her very close. His hand was spread warm across her back.

'I never really enjoyed those times. I was always so full of expectation.'

So I chaffed them and I gaily laughed to think they could doubt my love

And yet today my love has flown away

Turning and turning. A slight sigh as the needle gathers up the sound from so long ago.

I am without my love.

'I never quite knew what it was I expected . . . but it never happened anyway.'

'Kisses in the dark?'

'Even that seemed . . . well so run of the mill . . .' she laughed. 'Inept too, only you never liked to admit it.'

'I was never much good at the slow foxtrot.'

'I think we're doing very well, all things considered.'

So I smile and say

When a lovely flame dies

Smoke gets in your eyes.

He moved his cheek against hers and the sudden scratch of stubble made her heart thud. Oh no God, please God, don't let anything stupid happen.

The music stopped.

'A bit before your time, that one, I'd have thought,' he said.

'It was my absolute favourite when I was about fourteen. I think I must have stolen it from my parents.'

He held her still. She moved her head and looked at him.

'What'll we have next?' he asked.

The warm hand moved from her back.

'I'll wind, you choose,' she said.

'Slow, slow or quick, quick?' he asked.

'Anything except a tango. I never mastered the tango. I

always used to start laughing when you had to do those little rushes. This is fun.' The handle creaked as she turned it. 'Isn't it?'

He nodded.

'Glen Miller, Tommy Dorsey, Spike Jones and his City Slickers.' He handed her a record. She looked at the title before putting it on the turntable. *This is a Lovely Way to Spend an Evening*. She smiled.

'Sinatra, Crosby. I hated Crosby. The nurses used to play Crosby until I wanted to scream. Maybe I did scream. Maybe that's why they thought I was mad. Do you know I still think about those poor lunatics in the woods at Arnhem. Imagine being shut up for years and then suddenly finding that the walls had fallen down and that you were free. Free to wander in such a nightmare wood. If I could have painted, those would have been my pictures. I'm glad you don't have such pictures in your head.'

She pushed the switch and the record whirled. She put the needle gently down on the edge of the record. After a moment the music began.

'Shall we dance?' he asked.

She turned towards him.

'Yes.'

'We weren't going to play the remembering game.'

'No.'

'I'm sorry.'

'If it helps. . . .'

'It doesn't.'

They danced in silence. After a while she raised the hand that had been holding his empty shoulder and touched the destroyed face.

She thought it was going to alarm her, the feel of the dry cobbled skin, but to her fingers' surprise it was almost like running them over a canvas, grainy stretched parts and then densely textured paint, but warm like flesh should be, not canvas-cool.

The music stopped. The needle whirled and no sound came any longer to them as they stood close together in the middle of the room, her fingers gently touching his face.

'Please,' he said suddenly to her. 'Please, oh Helen, please.' His head drooped down onto her shoulder and he spoke the words into the angle of her neck.

'Helen. Please. Please. Helen.'

She moved her fingers to cover his smooth lips.

'Sssh. Yes,' she whispered.

He kissed her. Held her tight with his hand on her back so that she could feel his hardness. The stubble scratched, oh God, she thought again, where are You now? Why didn't You do something before it was too late?

It was half past eleven. Ten minutes later neither of them upstairs in his bedroom heard the lorry stop above the bend in the road, nor the steps of the two men from Ballybofey as they walked down the hill to the old level crossing gates. Quietly they opened the door of the goods shed. They shone the torch around the inside, into the corners, up to the roof and down again, round through the cobwebs and the dead flies the beams ranged. They didn't speak. They stepped out into the wind again and bolted the door behind them. They walked back up the hill and got into the lorry and drove away.

*

The sky was streaked with blue when she woke up the next morning. After a moment of puzzlement she remembered where she was and why she was there. His warm body was quite still beside her. She turned her head. His eye, a deeper, more constant blue than the sky, was looking at her.

'I must go.' She whispered the words as if the house were full of listening ears.

She scrambled out of the bed and began to pick up her clothes from the floor. He just lay there.

'Are you angry with me?' he asked at last, as she fumbled with the buttons on her skirt.

'No.'

He sighed.

'Why are you running away?'

'I'm not. I have to go. I mean, there's the cat, and I have to work, and the Aga needs filling and . . . and . . . oh no I'm not a bit angry.'

She moved round to his side of the bed and bent and kissed him gently on the cheek.

'I just have to hurry home.'

She went over to the door.

'You are a funny woman,' he said after her. 'I love you.'

She turned back and smiled at him.

'Thank you,' she said.

She hurried home.

The wind had almost calmed itself and the morning was silent. She could smell the sea tang and the drift of turf smoke from the village. She ran along the road, not running away, but running to her work.

The cat walked angrily past her when she opened the door.

'Silly cat,' she shouted after him.

She rattled out the Aga and filled it with anthracite, put the kettle on and went upstairs to change into her jeans. She looked at herself in the glass as she undressed.

'I must diet,' she said.

It was a passing thought rather than a decision.

She worked until the light began to drain away. She got up and turned on the light, rolled her head round and round, dislodging stiffness, stretched her arms. Hunger moved inside her. Carefully she lifted the canvas from the floor and propped it up beside the first one.

'Yes.'

She cleaned her brushes and stood them into the white enamel jug. She threw the dirty pieces of cloth into a box under the table. She emptied ash from the saucers and butts and broken matchsticks. Finally she laid a new canvas on the floor. Then she turned out the light and went across the yard to the house.

The kettle was sighing on the Aga.

The sound penetrated her mind after a few moments.

The cat was curled in the middle of the table.

That fact too became, after a moment, a puzzle.

The cat jumped onto the floor and rubbed its body round and round her ankles. 'Cat,' she said. She bent down and scratched his head. 'How on earth did you get in?' She listened to the kettle.

'Hello,' she called out. 'Who's here?'

Steps in the hall and Roger appeared in the doorway.

'I didn't want to disturb you,' he said.

She stared at him.

'I'm sorry,' she said after quite a long silence. 'I don't want to see anyone at the moment. My head is full of work . . . full of other things, not . . .' she gestured round the room. 'Not. . . .'

'My head is full of you.'

'Please, Roger, go away.'

'I'll make you a cup of tea. I put the kettle on. You're tired.'

'Yes, I'm tired. I don't want a cup of tea.'

That was a lie.

'A drink?'

She shook her head.

'Just . . . I don't want to see anyone. Anyone. I don't want to talk, explain, argue.'

'Helen. . . .'

'I want you to understand.'

He turned and went out into the hall. One of his shoes creaked.

'I'm sorry,' she shouted after him, rather half heartedly.

He walked out into the porch and opened the hall door. A little wind rustled along the hall floor.

'No umbrage, Roger. No . . .'

He closed the door.

She didn't move until she heard his car starting. Behind her the lid of the kettle tapped and water spat out onto the stove.

Why can't I be the right person at the right time? The bubble is broken.

She heard the shattering glass in her head.

She poured some water into the teapot and swirled it round as she walked over to the sink. The warmth penetrated through the earthenware to her hands.

His hand's warmth on her back.

He stirred my sleeping guts.

She tipped the water into the sink.

Yes.

She walked back to the Aga and took the tea caddy down from the shelf. Two spoonfuls, make it three. Make it strong enough to stand a spoon in. Was what happened last night love? Desperation? Alcohol?

Yes, really. Yes to all three.

Such pleasure . . . rich uncomplicated pleasure. Unsearched for, that was one of the good things.

Why the hell did he have to come round and burst my bubble?

She tipped the kettle forward and a stream of water flowed into the teapot.

I don't want to love anybody. I don't want the burden of other people's pain. My own is enough.

Dear God, why did you give us eyes to see so much pain?

She put the lid on the teapot and closed down the Aga.

Forget I ever said that, God, I'm just feeling neurotic. She smiled. As if the Old Bugger didn't know.

She took down a mug from the dresser and put it on the table.

Why do you whisper green grass?

We didn't dance to that tune.

Why tell the trees what aint so?

Whispering grass.

The trees don't need to know.

I am a bitch. That's really all there is to tell the trees.

OhOhOh.

Whispering grass. . . .

The tea was dark brown. She knew before she even tasted it that it was going to be quite, quite disgusting.

It is possible to enjoy loving.

Tannic acid, she had always been told, stripped the lining from your stomach.

'Hello,' said Roger, from the doorway. 'I came back.'

In silence she got another mug from the dresser.

'Have some unbelievably disgusting tea.'

'I'm sorry,' he said. 'I came back to say that. That's all.'

'Is it possible to enjoy loving?' she asked, as if he'd been in the room with her all the time.

'Yes,' he said. 'I think it is.' He moved silently back out through the door again. She heard no sound of steps, no door close, no car. She wondered after a few minutes if he had been there at all.

*

The man was moving out into the centre of the sea. His arms, like bird's wings poised now for swimming. Above in the sky, a gull, his echo, coasted. She worked quickly, hardly taking daylight time off for air or cups of tea. She didn't even smoke much, lit the odd cigarette, puffed, left it on a plate to burn itself out. Expensive, she thought once as she caught sight of the cylinders of ash lying side by side on the white china. A terror drove her on, the thought always in the back of her mind that she might not get the pictures finished. It was almost as if she herself might disintegrate, in half an hour, tomorrow, leaving nothing behind but an unfinished thought.

She slept restlessly, just waiting really for the light to come again, thinking or dreaming, she never knew which, of the mad people at Arnhem, lost among the trees and the young men falling from the sky. The sun and moon together watched as the young men fell. The cat, unperturbed by dreams, slept comfortably in the angle between her neck and shoulder. She tried to keep out of the dream, to keep her eyes open, to be aware of the cat's warm reality against her. But the trees, burdened yet with their dusty summer leaves crowded the room, their scarred limbs split, echoed men, limbs also split, silent, disturbing images. The demented moved with care through the trees, their ironic freedom full of danger.

'I actually don't have to put up with this,' she said. She sat up, pushing away the cat and the warm bedclothes, feeling on the floor with her feet for her slippers. To her surprise there was daylight coming through the window. The sun before seven touching the chairs and dressing table, the snap of Dan smiling in a silver frame. She wondered each time she caught sight of it why she didn't get rid of it. She didn't have to have him keeping an eye on her like this. It was probably the thought of having to explain his disappearance to Mrs O'Sullivan, who cleaned the silver frame once a week, that prevented her from disposing of the picture. Mrs O'Sullivan might consider any act of that kind to be akin to murder.

The cat yawned. One day I must get the elegant structure of that yawn onto paper. She tied her dressing gown around her and went downstairs.

*

That evening she went over to the house to find Damian re-hanging the kitchen door.

'Good heavens,' she said. 'What are you doing? Life is full of surprises.'

'I took about a quarter of an inch off the bottom of that for you. You'll find it works easier now. Don't mind the mess. I'll clear it up in a tick. Here, could you just steady this a minute till

I get the pins into the hinges.'

'This is really very kind of you. I'm sure you have other things you should be doing.'

'We have the first gate finished and hung. It looks great. I just have to give it a couple of coats of paint. We've been really hard at it the last couple of days. Otherwise I'd have been over to do this before. That's okay. You can let go now. See.'

He opened and shut the door a couple of times.

'I've given the hinges a taste of oil too.'

'Thank you, Damian. I. . . . Can I get you a drink?'

'Aye. That'd be great. Let you tell me where is the dustpan and I'll clear this mess and you go up and get dressed.'

She suddenly realised that she was still in her dressing gown.

'Oh God,' she said.

'He might come round. He said to ask you if that would be all right.'

'Yes. I've finished. I think I've finished the paintings. You'll have to come and see them. Yes. I'm glad he's coming. We can have a party. We can celebrate.'

'Why don't you go up and get dressed?'

'Yes.' She moved towards the stairs. 'Will you go and tell him?'

'No. He'll arrive.'

'I was so cross with him the other evening. . . .'

'Where's the dustpan?'

'Oh . . . in the cupboard . . . are you sure . . .?'

'Will you go and get dressed, woman. You look terrible. He'll be here otherwise.'

She rushed upstairs.

When she came down about half an hour later he was sitting at the table, looking at the paper. He grinned as she came into the room.

'That's better. You're a sight for sore eyes now.'

'I have sore eyes. I feel they're going to fall out of my head. A week in the Bahamas is what I'd like now. Just a long empty beach and warm sea. No bothers on me.'

'The beach would be packed. I've seen the crowds on the telly. Sharks would be waiting to bite your feet off. You're better off where you are.'

'Don't you believe it. Drinks by the pool served by handsome black men with shiny teeth. No newspapers. How the other half lives. Champagne for breakfast. I have wine or whisky, which would you prefer?'

'What are you having?'

'I think I'll have a glass of wine, but you don't have to have the same.'

He hesitated.

'Whisky,' she said for him.

'Okay.'

'Come into the other room. I see no reason why we should confine ourselves to the kitchen. Put some water in a jug, I'll just put a match to the fire.' When he followed her into the sitting room she was kneeling on the floor beside the fire. Early flames flickered through the sticks and coal. Smoke was just beginning to be drawn up into the chimney. She waved her hand towards a table in the corner of the room.

'Help yourself, and me please. I'll have a glass of red wine. And a gasper.' She felt in the pocket of her skirt. 'It's days since I had a proper smoke. Are you still saintly?'

'Yes.'

There was a burst of energy in the fire and the sticks began to crackle.

'You seem a very solitary sort of person,' she said. 'Don't you have friends? Don't you do things with friends? Brothers? I never see you around with people of your own age.'

'I do what pleases me.'

He crossed the room and handed her a glass of wine.

'Thank you. Sit down. The room'll warm up quickly.'

He sat in an armchair by the fire looking down at her, his glass held awkwardly out in front of him.

'Well,' she said. 'Here's health.' She held up her glass and smiled. 'Mud in your eye.' They both drank.

'No girl friend?'

'Girls come and go.'

'Lots of young men of your age are married.'

'Aye. The most of my friends. I don't feel like settling you know. I want to make my boat. You've no peace with a wife and kids.'

'Love, comfort, companionship? What about those sort of things?'

'I've never come across a girl yet I've felt I'd like to spend fifty years with. It's the settling worries me. There's all the time in the world for that. Later. My mother'd like to see me married. Get me off her hands.'

'Most people rush in to it too quickly. I did myself. It's hard to rush out again if it doesn't work.'

'Another couple of weeks now and we'll start on the boat. I have enough money put by for the timber. We're going to take the electricity over to the goods shed and we can work there during the winter. Then in the spring, when the weather starts to get better we're going to lay the tracks. . . .'

'How do you lay tracks? You and Roger can't lay tracks. It takes a whole gang of men to lay tracks.'

'In the spring we're going to lay the tracks,' he repeated.

She sighed.

'I think perhaps that was when he got into trouble last time,' said Damian.

'How do you mean?'

'In Scotland, or wherever it was. He started to have rows then with the railway people and his family got roped in to it all. It was bad trouble. I don't know why people won't just leave him alone.'

'I suppose he annoys them.'

'You wouldn't want to see him harmed, would you?'

'No.'

He smiled at her.

'I didn't think you would.'

She leant over and put some wood on the fire.

'Do you want to come and see the pictures?'

'Yes. My fame.'

'Come on then.' She pushed herself up from the floor and led him out across the yard.

The four canvases were standing against the wall. In the fourth painting the beach and the sea were empty expanses. A seagull moved across the glare of the sun and footprints displaced the sand, leading from a pile of clothes to the edge of the sea. The clothes were the only colourful objects in the four paintings. A red jersey thrown on top of faded blue jeans, a blue shirt, red and white striped runners, grey woollen socks to one side of the pile.

'Where am I?' he asked. 'What have you done with me?' His

voice sounded slightly panic stricken, as if she had disposed of his reality in some way.

'You've gone.'

'But why? Why did I have to go? Couldn't I come back again?'

She laughed.

He examined the clothes closely, stooping down to study them.

'They're mine all right,' he said. 'I must be going to come back. God, Helen, that's a creepy thing to do to someone. Make them disappear like that.'

He clicked his fingers.

'Well,' she said. 'Not quite like that. You can see from the beginning that he's going to disappear.'

'He?'

'You, if you like.'

He looked at each one in turn again.

'Yes, I suppose you can.'

'You just have to forget that it's you, Damian. If it upsets you.'

He nodded.

'What are you going to call them?'

'Rather boring really. "Man on a Beach."'

'That's all?'

'1, 2, 3, 4.'

'Helen.'

Roger's voice called across the yard.

'Here,' she called back.

'Man on a Beach, Man in the Sea, Man Swimming and A Pile of Lonely Clothes would be better names,' suggested Damian.

Roger's lurching steps crossed the yard.

'Man on a Beach. Like it or lump it,' said Helen.

The door opened and Roger came in.

'I've finished.'

'The Short Story of Disappearing Damian.'

'Pay no attention to him,' said Helen.

Roger looked at the pictures in silence. Helen watched his face for a while and then turned away and began to tidy up things on the table. Pencils, brushes, into neat rows, smallest to the left. She scraped at the clotted paint on the blade of a knife with her finger nail.

'Yes,' he said at last. 'It's finished.'

She put the knife down on the table.

'I . . . well . . . what do you think?'

'I think you are a most remarkable woman.'

'The painting. . . .'

'To have held all that inside you for so long, without driving yourself into some state of insanity. Looking at that, one would think you'd been painting for years.'

'I have. In my head.'

He took her hand and kissed it.

'Hey,' said Damian. 'She's made me disappear and you kiss her hand. That's my fame there and look what she does to me.'

She linked her arm through his.

'I'll paint you building your boat. How will that be?'

'No more disappearing?'

'No. Solid as a rock.'

'Okay.'

'Let's go. Let's have a happy time.'

They crossed the yard to the house, linked together not merely with their arms, but by an exuberant peacefulness.

Three people are happy, she thought, as she pulled the curtains tight almost as if to keep out the world's unhappiness. That's a crazy sentimental thought if there ever was one. She wondered if she could have ever felt this way with Dan and Jack. There had been too much judging. How strange. I was happy when I started to pull the curtains and now here I am, as I finish that act, melancholy once more. A passing melancholy, that's all I intend it to be.

'What's the cat's name?'

'Sorry.'

She turned from the curtains and looked towards them. Damian was leaning over the back of the sofa scratching the cat's stretched orange stomach.

'I've brought some champagne,' said Roger. 'But it's the one thing I can't manage. It's in the kitchen. I'll just. . . .' He went out of the room.

'He doesn't have a name.'

'Why not? I've never heard of a pet before without a name.'

'Dogs, yes. A dog without a name would be a lost soul, but cats are different. "I am the cat who walked by myself and all places are alike to me." I think you diminish a cat by calling it

Tommy or Smudge or something . . . anyway they come if you call puss, puss, so why bend your mind any further than that. He's puss puss at meal times and bloody cat when I'm angry with him.' The cat twitched his ears at the familiar words.

'You win,' said Damian. 'I'll never call a cat Tommy or Smudge.'

Roger came back with one bottle in his hand and another tucked awkwardly under his arm.

'Oh what a beautiful sight,' said Helen. 'I don't think I have the right glasses. I hope you don't mind.'

'I've never tasted champagne,' said Damian.

'The great cure all. Here.' Roger put one bottle on the table and handed Damian the other one. 'The doctors' surgeries would be empty if only more people were aware of its magic qualities. Glasses at the ready, Helen? Lesson number one. Take off the paper and then unscrew the wire. Right. Hold it carefully and then with both thumbs ease the cork. The right hand over the top. That's it. Feel it coming?'

Damian nodded.

'Glass, Helen. It shouldn't pop too hard. A well pulled champagne cork should just jump quietly into your hand. That's it. Great.'

Helen caught the bubbles as the cork came away. Damian filled three glasses.

'Man on a Beach.' Roger raised his glass.

'Man on a Beach.'

'Me,' said Damian.

They drank.

'That's lovely. You didn't get that down in Mr Hasson's Hotel.'

'I did not. What do you think, Damian? As good as a pint of Smithwicks?'

'I think I could learn to love it, given a bit of practise.'

'That's good. Mind you, you can get ghastly stuff. Sweet, like sparkling eau de cologne. Knappogue Road.' He drank again.

'Knappogue Road,' said Helen. Might as well, she thought, it's his champagne.

'Aye,' said Damian. 'The station.'

*

'I suppose we should eat,' said Helen about an hour later. 'I think I may only have eggs.'

'I love eggs,' said Roger.

Damian stood up.

'I'd better be going.'

'Don't be silly. Why would you go? Sit down, Damian. We're all going to eat eggs. . . .'

'My mother'll have saved my tea.'

'It will be disgusting now.'

'I think. . . .'

'If you really want to.'

'Yes.'

Roger groped in his pocket and took out his keys. He held them out to Damian.

'Here. Take the car. I'm going to be in no fit state to drive. Just mind it. Mind yourself.'

Damian took the keys.

'Thank you. Yes. Thank you.'

He did a little bow to each of them in turn.

'Tomorrow.'

He went out jingling the keys in his hand.

'Well,' said Helen after a moment.

'Well what?'

'A trifle high handed perhaps?'

'Not at all. I simply thought I didn't want to give the postman, nice as he is, the fun of seeing my car outside your door at eight o'clock in the morning.'

'You're making assumptions. . . . Anyhow I never get any post.'

'Am I?'

'Omelettes,' she said, standing up. 'Scrambled, poached, boiled. . . .'

'Am I, Helen?'

'Fried, coddled. . . .'

'Helen.'

'Take your pick. Yes. You're making assumptions . . . but they're correct. I expected you to stay the night. Even if you hadn't brought the champagne I'd have expected you to stay the night. I'll even go so far as to say that I want you to stay the night.'

He smiled.

'What's a coddled egg? That's a new one on me.'

He got up and followed her into the kitchen.

'Good heavens, did you never have coddled eggs when you were a child?' She took a bowl of eggs from the top of the refrigerator and put them on the table.

'Almost hard boiled and then broken into a cup and sort of mushed around with lots of butter and pepper and salt. Then you eat it with fingers of toast. Maybe it wouldn't be nice now. Oh dear, that's a really nostalgic memory. Nursery tea, and our pyjamas warming on the guard in front of the fire. How peaceful and safe it seemed.'

'I don't think we'll have our eggs coddled. Apart from the fact that you would obviously drown in sentimentality, I've brought a nice bottle of claret. An omelette would be the most suitable dish on offer.'

'You seem to have a bottomless well of wine up there.'

'I see no reason to deprive myself of the good things of life, just because I choose to live separately.'

She took a bowl from the dresser and began to crack eggs into it.

'What would you have done, Roger, if . . . if . . . things had been different? If Arnhem hadn't happened?'

'I think the Bar and then perhaps politics was what they had in mind for me.'

'What did you have in mind for yourself?'

'I did not have time to find out. Those last couple of years at school I actually didn't care who won as long as the war ended before I had to get out there and fight. My head was full of such patriotic thoughts,' he laughed. 'I remember saying that to my father one night. I thought he was going to kill me on the spot. After that I kept my nasty thoughts to myself and just used to pray that I would be killed quickly. So you see I didn't have much time to work out what I wanted to do with my life.'

'To be serious. . . .'

She mixed the eggs together with a knife, tilting the bowl sideways as she worked.

'Oh I suppose I'd have liked to have been a writer, a painter, a poet, but I didn't have the gift. Nothing else ever seemed worthwhile to me. That's serious, Helen. I have left no footmark on the world. Three railway stations and a whole lot of angry relations . . . a great legacy.'

'Lay the table for me. You're starting to sound sorry for yourself.'

'No. I promise you, not that. I have enjoyed my railway stations and I'm embarrassed to say I've also enjoyed teasing my family . . . and I look forward to death. So . . . no sorrow. No happiness either. Just equilibrium.'

'You'll get knives and forks in the drawer behind you. I don't know what you're talking about at all. You've got less equilibrium than anyone I've ever met. Do you like herbs in your omelette?'

'Of course. Do you love me?'

She burst out laughing. She threw the knife across the room, clattering it into the metal sink. She picked up the bowl and walked with it in her hand over to the Aga. She stood there a moment with her back to him, before reaching to the cupboard for a small black iron pan.

'I don't know,' she said at last.

'I suppose that's not too bad an answer.'

He was meticulously spacing the knives and forks, the round rush mats, the wine glasses.

'Why do you wear your shirt in bed?' she asked.

'I would have thought the answer to that was obvious.'

'I'm not exactly a thing of beauty. Aren't those things forgettable?'

'Mutilation is an indignity. I like to preserve what dignity I can. It's pride, I'm afraid, Helen. Will you allow me that?'

'Yes. I'll allow you pride. Do you like your omelette runny in the middle?'

'No. Eggs should be hard.'

He poured them each a glass of wine.

*

It was the cat who woke Helen in the morning. Having jumped on to the bed, as was his custom, fairly early every morning, and found his pillow space to be occupied, he sat himself on Helen's chest and proceeded to stare morosely down at her face. After a few minutes she opened her eyes and stared back into the yellow ones that were staring at her. Beyond his head she could see blue sky through the window, the white frame reflected the hard glitter of the sun and a million dusty particles seemed caught in the morning light. Amazing, she thought how that one shaft of sun creates reality and mystery at the same time. Hard edge solidity at the window, then diffused, nothing defined any more, objects almost shimmering further into the room. Everywhere pools of dark. The cat bent forward and rubbed his head on her face. She disentangled a hand from the bedclothes and scratched at the top of his head.

'I suppose breakfast is in your mind, crude cat,' she said.

'Breakfast is in my mind too,' said Roger's voice from beside her.

She was startled.

'Had you forgotten about me?' he asked 'So soon? *La donna é mobile.*'

She laughed.

'No, no, no. I hope you haven't been awake for long thinking about breakfast.'

'Just a few minutes. The cat and I have had a small confrontation. I don't think he likes me.'

'He's just confused. He's a creature of habit. You're in his space. What time is it anyway?'

She looked at his watch.

'Eight.'

'Late. I'm usually up long before this. I've usually had two cigarettes by eight.'

'Well, I've at least saved you from that.'

'True. But on the other hand, the Aga may have gone out. It's also a creature of habit. It likes to breakfast at half past seven. . . .'

She began to hustle herself out of bed. He put his hand on her shoulder, holding her.

'Don't go.'

'I must.'

'Rubbish. Let the bloody Aga go out. Stay here with me. After all. . . .'

She shrugged his hand off her shoulder and got out of the bed.

'No.' Her voice was faintly exasperated.

The cat jumped down from the bed and rubbed himself around her bare legs.

'Even for Paul Newman I wouldn't let the Aga go out.'

She took her dressing gown from the back of the door and

put it on. The cat dashed out onto the small landing and waited at the top of the stairs for her to follow. She hunted round on the floor for something to put on her feet. The rope soles were under the bed. She bent down to pull them out. His fingers grappled into her hair.

'You're being very unromantic,' he said.

'I'm too old to be romantic.'

She shuffled her feet into the shoes and stood up.

He lay there already looking abandoned.

'There's too little time,' she said. 'Far too little time.'

She almost ran out of the room and tripped over the cat outside the door and they both fell several steps before she grabbed the bannister and landed angry and undignified half-way down the stairs. The cat fled round the corner and into the kitchen.

'Bloody cat,' she yelled after it.

'Are you all right?' Roger called from the bedroom.

'No bones broken. Dignity impaired. Suffering from mild shock. Blood pressure going crazy. Otherwise everything all right.'

'It's a judgment on you for being unromantic. What's so great about Paul Newman anyway?'

He stood in the doorway looking down at her, the bed-spread draped around him. She stood up slowly, creaking and crackling like a pair of cheap shoes.

'Just the glorious unattainable.' She began to laugh. 'You look like a Roman senator. Heroic and noble.'

'And crumbling. One half of the face removed by the worms of time and weather. I like the idea.'

One of her shoes was at the bottom of the stairs. She hobbled down and put her foot into it.

'Do you want a bath?'

'Roman senators spent their time having baths.'

'You'll find towels in the press in the bathroom. There'll be breakfast in about half an hour. Ave atque vale.'

'Miaow,' screeched the hungry cat.

Aga revived, the cat content and asleep on the chair in the porch, they sat, almost accustomed to each other at the kitchen table, eating toast. He was amazingly adept, she thought. He seemed to be able to cope more neatly with his one hand than she had ever managed to with two.

'Did you never think to have an attachment of some sort . . . a false arm . . . you know?'

'I tried. Yes. Years ago. When I was still in hospital. They all thought it would make life much easier for me. I found it a bit repulsive though. Things might be different now, but then, what they offered me was quite crude and . . . well . . . repulsive is the best word I can think of. A lot of straps and things.' He smiled. 'I was allowed out one weekend to stay with my father and I went off for a walk and dropped the damn thing in the river. They were quite cross really. All of them. Yes. Quite cross. They considered I was ungrateful. I thought that was funny. There was a lot of trouble round about then.'

'What sort of trouble?'

'Trouble.' He looked vague. 'Prison and that sort of thing.'

'Prison? You've never been in prison, Roger. What on earth are you talking about?'

'It was prison all right. I wanted to go to Oxford. I had it all set up. They made allowances in those days for chaps like . . . injured . . . you know . . . allowances.'

He looked past her out of the window, his eye, reflective, had lots its blue energy.

'I could have managed.'

'I'm sure you could.'

'I wanted to be shown how to start my head working. I knew I had to do that before I could do anything else. No, they said. Damn it all, I'd passed those exams at school. Place all ready waiting when you come back from the war, they said. I could have managed.'

She was making a ring of cigarettes on the table, each one standing upright like a soldier, on its filter end.

'No, they said. You're not fit yet. Not fit to look after yourself. Not fit. When you're fit we'll reconsider. So, it was prison.'

'Not prison,' she said, keeping her eyes on the cigarettes. 'You told me yourself, a nursing home.'

'Genteel bars at my window, so that I couldn't throw myself out. A shadow always there, always walking behind me, watching me read, eat, sleep. I wasn't even allowed to lock the bathroom door. The degrees of comfort are irrelevant, the disciplines are irrelevant. A prison is always a prison.'

'What had you done to them?'

'I hadn't done anything. They just wanted me to be normal. Fit. Fit to be taken about in polite society. Our hero son. Polite, hero, son. Heroes should be grateful for the passing admiration in the eyes of others. Grateful for a pension. Grateful for the small attentions we throw to them. Grateful to be alive. I didn't want to fit in or to be fit. So they thought it was best to shut me up somewhere. They used to tell me how much money they were spending on me.'

He smiled again. The scar beneath his eye patch puckered with the strain.

She saw it suddenly in terms of textures, painful colours mixed on the palette. A line of light ran from the black patch down to the jaw.

'It was my money. They had nothing to complain about.'

'That's over, a long time ago,' she said gently.

'No. Now at this moment perhaps I'm free from the ghosts. But any moment, without any warning, Helen, they take over my mind . . . and my body. Pain and ghosts. I become imprisoned again.'

'Those are all images of the past. I'm inept at this sort of conversation. It's all over now. Stop conjuring up nightmares. Leave the past alone. That will be your freedom.'

He said nothing for a long time. Little pulses beat beside his eye and in his throat.

'Why are you doing that with the cigarettes?' he asked at last, his voice normal.

She flipped her hand and the standing cigarettes fell down. She began to put them back into the box.

'I get quite nervous,' she said. 'When people talk. I talk so seldom to other people. I feel disadvantaged. It wasn't inattention, I assure you.' She laughed. 'Like Mrs Hasson, I suffer from nerves. Luckily no exeema, just straightforward nerves.'

He stood up suddenly, the tension gone miraculously from his face. 'Up, up, woman. Go and dress yourself. I'm going back to the station to collect the car and have a word with Damian and then we'll go and have our picnic at the Devil's Well. Tobar na . . . whatever you call it.'

*

There was no strong west wind blowing. The flat rocks were dry, the reflections in the narrow pools were without movement. Through the mirrored sky you could see clearly the sloping sides covered with barnacles and wisps of weed. Limpets clung just below the surface of the water and a discarded claw from some tiny crab lay among the pebbles on the bottom of one pool. She wondered how she could translate to canvas the opaque mystery of reflection imposed on the reality of granite, weed and shell. Odd, she thought, I've always looked through the reflection in the past, disregarded that dimension. Such blindness. Untrained eyes.

He took her arm and they walked to the edge of the blowing hole and looked down. Far below them, in the darkness, water plocked, glittered for a moment and was still, plocked again.

'When Damian's boat is finished,' said Roger, 'we'll get him to bring us close in, to see the entrance to the cave. It must be very low down, totally covered, I'd say, at high tide. I wonder why they called it the Devil's Well? It's not a well at all.'

'It looks like one from here. Those smooth sides look almost man-made. It's not till you see it in action that you realise what it is. A spout. The Devil's Spout would have been a better name. Wouldn't it?'

She bent down and picked up a small stone and wondered whether to drop it into the hole. She decided against that traditional gesture and instead turned away from Roger and walked to the edge of the rocks. She threw the stone out into the sea and watched while it dropped out of her sight. A gull, interested for a moment, changed course, floated down almost to the water and then without any apparent effort rose back to its original flight path once more.

'I get vertigo,' shouted Roger. 'I always have the terrible temptation to jump from heights.'

She moved back from the edge towards him.

'It would be such an exciting way to die. They say you become unconscious quite quickly, so you wouldn't feel the nasty bit at the end. You'd just fly out of life. That appeals to me.'

'Too nice a day for morbid thoughts,' Helen said. She stared down at the flat rocks.

'Do you think these rocks are neolithic?'

'I haven't the faintest idea what they might be.'

'"Of or belonging to the later stone age." That's what the dictionary says. Not much help. I did some paintings of them and wondered whether I could call them neolithic or not. The OED is usually more helpful than that.'

'That's probably helpful enough if you know the difference between the later stone age, the early stone age, the bronze age, the ice age. I'd use the word neolithic if it pleases you, if it seems right.'

'I'd better not. Some elderly geologist would be bound to complain.'

She bent down and stirred in a shallow pool with her hand.

'Will you marry me, Helen?'

Oh damn, she thought, straightening up, shaking the drops from her fingers. The tiny stains dried almost at one, leaving the rocks unblemished.

'Helen.'

He was just behind her.

She was suddenly conscious of a lark's song spiralling above her and she stared up into the sky, trying to catch sight of the moving bird. Roger spoke her name again, a foreground to the distant warbling.

'No,' she said.

'Did you hear what I asked you?'

'Yes.'

She turned round and looked at him.

'Thank you. Yes, I heard. Thank you very much, but no.'

'Why not?'

She laughed a little.

'Men always ask why not.'

'I mean, is it because of the way I am . . . physically? Is that it?'

'No.'

'I love you, Helen. I never thought I'd find myself in this position. I never thought I'd find anyone that. . . . I never thought I could love anyone. Perhaps we could be happy, Helen.'

He picked up her left hand and held it to the whole side of his face. It felt almost feverish, she thought.

How unkind of God to dangle the prospect of happiness in front of me at this moment in my life.

They stood in silence for a moment. The lark continued to sing.

'You don't love me,' he said at last.

'I do. I promise you I do.' She took a step forward and leaned her head on his chest.

'Why, then?'

'I want to own myself.'

'Darling, it won't be like that. I swear. I don't want to take anything away from you. I only want to give you whatever you want. Everything.'

'I only want one thing, you know.'

'I know what you're going to say . . . freedom. Isn't that right? I'll give you freedom.'

'I don't want you to give me anything. I want my own space. A little bit of time. I don't want anyone to give me anything. All that kindness, all that giving that you talk about, offer me, it could be like a prison. Couldn't it? I'd rather love you outside that. I haven't the energy for another marriage, Roger. Please try to understand.'

She rubbed at his cheek with her fingers. She smiled.

'I'd say the same thing to Paul Newman.'

He pulled himself away from her and walked across the rocks back towards the lane where the car was parked.

'Bloody man,' she shouted after him, as if he were the cat. 'Why don't you understand? I thought at least that you would understand. That's one reason I love you. Because . . . you should . . . you. . . .'

He walked away.

Tears filled her head.

The lark was quite unperturbed.

The sea, the rocks, crumpled and splintered with the tears in her eyes.

I will not cry, she said. Not cry after any person who doesn't understand.

'Hail to thee blithe spirit,' she shouted into the splintering sky.

'Bird thou never wert

That from heaven or near it – '

The danger receded. The world came once more into her own peculiar focus. The bird flickered in the light, remained in her eye's sight.

'Pourest thy full heart in profuse strains of unpremeditated art.'

Flick, flick.

'That's what comes of sleeping through all those years of expensive education. You can't get beyond the fourth line of one of the world's classics.'

Bastún. Ignoramus. Layabout.

She sat on the edge of a rock and felt in her pockets for the cigarettes.

Or was it perhaps the fifth line?

She heard his step on the rocks.

'I've forgotten the rest,' she said.

He carried the thermos flask under his arm and in his hand her cigarettes. 'There's a bit about harmonious madness. I never liked Shelley.'

She looked alarmed.

'Keats. Surely. "Ode to the Skylark" is Keats, isn't it?'

He sat down beside her with a heavy graceless thump.

'Shelley. Nightingale Keats, skylark Shelley. I'm sorry, Helen. I didn't mean to be insensitive. Here. I've brought your poison . . . and the coffee.'

She took the box and the matches from him and put them in her pocket.

He put the flask between his knees and unscrewed the top. He handed the top to her and then filled it with coffee. Her hand was shaking and the liquid swirled up to the edge and back to the centre again. She ducked her head down towards her hand and sucked some coffee into her mouth. It was black, sweet, laced with whisky.

'Oh, that's good.'

She drank some more and handed him the cup.

'A loving cup,' she said.

He took a drink and put the cup down on the rock beside him. He picked up her hand and kissed it.

'I only thought that perhaps we could push a bit of loneliness away. Yours as well as mine.'

His mouth moved against her fingers.

The lark had now moved so far away that she could barely hear it.

'No,' she said. 'Time. Perhaps if we'd been young there would have been time for everything. I don't think so. You think that all time is there before you. Lovely empty time. If you're not very careful your past is empty time too and you have nothing to recognise yourself by. That nearly happened to me. Only a cruel accident stopped it happening to me. A cruel miracle maybe.'

The sky was now silent.

'I have so many questions to ask, Roger. Ask and ask and ask.'

He passed her the cup of coffee.

'Thanks.'

She took a drink, and then another and then handed the cup to him.

'That's all,' she said. 'That's the only reason. It's to do with me, not you.'

He looked silently at the cup in his hand. Tiny freckles patterned his wrist. She wondered how she had never noticed them before.

'Marriage isn't a cure for loneliness anyway. Sometimes it makes it more painful. I suppose some sort of close relationship with God is the only real answer to that. How absurd we are on such a day to be so melancholy.'

'Yes.'

'We can enjoy what we have, you know. There's nothing to stop us doing that. Darling, Roger, thank you so much for your generosity. I'm just sorry I can't be equally generous in return. But let's enjoy what we've got.'

She was wearing those damn shoes again and dampness was seeping through to her feet. Will you never learn sense? Dan had always been so right in the things he said to her.

'Will you let me take you away somewhere . . . just a couple of weeks . . . a holiday . . . that sort of thing?'

'Yes. I'd love that. As soon as I get my pictures up to Dublin, weather that storm. Yes.'

He smiled at last. He finished the coffee in the cup and poured some more into it from the flask.

'It struck me the other day,' he said, handing her the coffee. 'That we should go to Florence. You shouldn't spend the rest of your life here painting neolithic rocks without having been to Florence. It would give me great, great pleasure to be with you in that particular city.'

'Oh, yes. Such a beautiful prospect. Let's go home and light the fire and make plans. I love making plans.'

She stood up and held out a hand to him.

'And make love?'

'Of course.'

She pulled him up.

'My feet are wet. Cold. Think of all the lovely Italian shoes I can buy. I'll be able to throw all my clompers away.'

He laughed.

She bent down and picked up the flask and the top.

'Loving cup again.'

She took a long drink and handed it to him. He finished it. She screwed it on to the top of the flask.

'Are you sure about Shelley?' she asked.

'Quite sure.'

*

The miles drove by under their wheels.

As before, Manus didn't speak, though this time he was awake, his eyes open staring out through the windscreen of the car.

It was the old situation of the right hand not letting the left hand know what it was doing. Presumably Manus had been organising the thing for days. If I followed in my mother's footsteps, I'd now be devouring the cigarettes, stick after stick. From time to time Manus broke a piece of chocolate from a bar in his pocket and put it into his mouth. Never offered it around. He must have had about a dozen bars softening away in there. Amazing he didn't ever feel the need to puke.

He'd been standing outside the Arts block when Jack had come out of his last lecture and had followed him across Front Square to his rooms.

'Right,' he said, as Jack put his papers down on the table. 'We're off.'

'Off where?'

'Donegal. Come on. I've been hanging around for the last hour waiting for you.'

'I'm supposed to be going to my grandmother tonight.'

'Ring her,' said Manus. 'And get a move on. The lads are waiting beyond Maynooth with the stuff in a truck.'

'You mean . . . ?'

'Don't ask any questions, because I'm not answering them. Here's money for petrol.'

He took six fivers from his pocket and handed them to Jack. 'Now ring your fucking granny and let's go.'

Half an hour later on the road heading out of Dublin, Jack spoke.

'What am I supposed to do?'

'Drive.'

'Don't be damn silly. When we get there? What then?'

'We'll see when we get there. There may be no call for you to do anything but sit in the car and drive me home again.'

'It all seems a bit undefined to me.'

'What does that mean?'

That was when he took the first bar from his pocket, Cadbury's Fruit and Nut, a meal in itself. He snapped a row off the bar and dropped the paper on the floor between his feet.

'Casual. Unplanned. Liable to fall apart at the seams.'

'When I want your opinion I'll ask for it. Just drive.'

He shoved the chocolate angrily into his mouth.

Jack drove.

Kilcock, Mullingar, Langford, Carrick on Shannon, Boyle, interminable flat miles.

From time to time Manus turned his head and stared out the back window, checking that the lorry was still behind them. Outside Killucan, Jack had drawn into a petrol station and he had watched the lorry drive past them, two men in the cab. He wondered what their load consisted of. Manus ate more chocolate. Through the town and the lorry pulled off the verge and fell in behind them again.

As it began to get dark, Manus spoke.

'Don't drive too fast. Don't make it hard for them. We don't want the buggers getting lost.'

Silence.

I wonder why I do this. I get no satisfaction, no glory . . . just an aching bum. What am I trying to do? Right some ancient wrong? Come, come, surely not that. Cancel out in some way the labels they hand on me . . . West Brit, shoneen, bourgeois? Show them . . . whoever they may be, that my heart is in the right place? He drove a car for fifty thousand miles for Ireland. Got blisters on his arse for Ireland and a first-class degree to please his grandmother . . . with a bit of luck. Some curriculum vitae that. Menial tasks for Ireland. What about the dead? The sad? The suffering? You can't make an omelette without, ha ha, breaking eggs. I have my own dead.

My mother sat alone all those evenings. She never held my hand. I could run this whole damn outfit a million times better than Manus, with his devious ways and his bars of chocolate. This operation for instance. No plans . . . just a vague hope of muddling through. We'll see what happens when the moment comes. Apart from the Englishman and my mad mother there's Damian to contend with. Maybe I just conjure up difficulties. Have too much imagination, like Manus said. Officers should only see what will happen, not what might happen. Stick to driving cars, Jackson Cuffe, certainly until you have your motives sorted out.

'Easy. Slow down. Easy through Sligo. Who do you think you are? Stirling Moss?'

Motives.

Could we look at the possibility of creating a situation where the blabbing mouths of the political posturers were silenced once and for all? That, as Shakespeare said, is a consummation devoutly to be wished. Worth getting blisters on your backside for.

But. Oh but, but, but, is it worth, ha ha, breaking eggs for? I often wonder to myself why I don't use that brisk word . . . kill. It makes me feel uneasy, that's why. Manus has a gun on his person. Manus has no scruples. Does he really have a dream, or merely no scruples?

I would think that I am probably driving across Ireland with a chrysalis beside me. One day, he too, like so many others with no scruples, will emerge, blossom from his chrysalis state into a free flying political posturer. For that it is not worth getting blisters on your. . . .

Do I really have to do this to prove my identity?

Or am I just too lazy to do it any other way?

Why was I born with a silly name like Jackson Cuffe around my neck?

If my father hadn't been shot and I hadn't been the recipient of a considerable sum of compensation, I wouldn't have a car in which to drive Manus interminably silent miles. What then? What other menial task would they have entrusted to me?

I depress myself at times.

'Pull up here, for a minute or two. I want to piss and have a couple of words with the lads.'

Jack drew in to the side of the road and stopped. The lorry stopped about twenty yards behind them. Manus got out of the car and walked back along the road.

Jack opened the door of the car and got out to stamp the stiffness from his bones. It was very cold and starry bright. The huge flint sprinkled sky hung silent above him. His hands were silver, the road, the low thorn hedge and the hills, quite silver, naked, nowhere to hide. He could smell the sea, hear though no sound, only the low voices of the three men talking secrets.

He got back in the car and banged the door closed to dispel the unease that came to him sometimes with night silence. The inside of the car smelt disagreeable. He rolled down the window and waited until he heard Manus' footsteps returning along the road, then he put out his hand and started the engine.

Manus settled himself into his seat and groped for chocolate.

'That's okay,' he said. 'Want a piece?' He offered a bar of Kit-Kat in Jack's direction.

'No thanks.'

'I've told them to give us twenty minutes. That's in case your man is around.'

'If he is?'

Manus dropped the paper on the floor and began to eat the chocolate. 'That's your problem. You'll think up something to get him out of the way. If that happens, if we're seen . . . or rather if you're seen, you'll have to spend a couple of days with your mother. I'll go back to Dublin with the boys in the lorry.'

'What'll I say to her? She'll be extremely amazed to see me.'

'You'll think of something. Move it.'

'Sure they won't get lost?' asked Jack, jerking his head backwards towards the lorry.

'If they get lost, I'll have their balls.'

There was no light, no movement at the station. Jack stopped the car and Manus got out.

'It's a bugger of a night. You could hear the grass growing and see it too.'

Jack nodded.

'Get on down anyway and see if he's at the house. If he is we're elected.' He looked at his watch. 'Give us half an hour minimum. That's fifteen minutes. . . . and half an hour. . . . keep him occupied till ten thirty. I'll see you back in Dublin.'

'If he's not there?'

'Don't go in. Come back up here and park the car outside the door. If he comes back it'll be up to you to occupy his mind. I'd say he'd be at the house below.'

He closed the car door quietly and pointed down the hill. Jack nodded and drove off.

They lay on the sofa in front of the fire, half drunk with love and wine. The flickering light from the fire made their bodies seem to writhe, but they were in fact quite still, quite peaceful. They heard nothing but the sound of their own breathing, the pumping of two hearts. They heard no car, no latch click, no steps in the hall. The first moment they were aware of Jack's presence was when he opened the sitting-room door and switched on the light.

'Mother . . . oh Jesus God!'

Helen stared, confused across the back of the sofa for what seemed like a long time before she gathered into her mind what was happening.

'Jack.'

She stood up, fastening the buttons down the front of her shirt.

'You never told me you were coming down.'

She bent and picked her skirt from the floor and stepped into it.

Roger sat up, rubbing at his eye as if it were paining him.

'Hello, Jack.' His voice was composed.

Helen picked up his trousers and dropped them on top of him.

'You should have let me know you were coming. I think we've probably eaten all the food.'

'I don't need food. I tried to phone but I couldn't get through,' he lied.

She nodded, not believing him.

'I think I'll just . . .' He backed out of the room into the hall . . . 'just, bathroom.'

He disappeared and they heard him running up the stairs. Roger got up from the sofa and pulled his trousers on.

'I suppose we've shocked him,' said Helen. 'Oh dear . . . I hope we haven't appalled him.' She giggled. 'His face was appalled. I hope he doesn't do anything awful up there.'

'Don't be silly, Helen, he'll just recover his equilibrium and then he'll come down. You'd better give him a large drink.'

Helen was punching at the cushions on the sofa.

'Is this sordid?' she asked, suddenly anxious, 'or really a bit funny? It's not very dignified.'

'It would have been one hell of a lot less dignified if he'd arrived ten minutes earlier. A whisky? I'm having a whisky. To induce the correct light-hearted approach.'

'I'll stick to wine.'

Jack came into the room.

'Whisky?' asked Roger. Jack nodded abruptly and walked over to Helen who was standing with her back to the fire.

'What's all this anyway?'

'What's all what?'

'This . . . this. . . .' He pointed towards the sofa.

'Have your drink, Jack dear. There's no need for you to get all worked up.'

'I'm not worked up.'

Roger came across the room and put a glass of whisky into his hand.

'I'm embarrassed. I'm ashamed. For God's sake, I might have had someone with me.'

'But you didn't,' said Helen. 'And anyway if you'd said you were coming down we would have behaved in a more appropriate way.'

'Would you mind very much opening this bottle of wine for your mother? I can't use this corkscrew.'

'Yes, I do mind. My mother's had enough to drink all ready. I can see that by looking at her.'

'You're being a bit grotesque,' said Helen, coldly.

'Grotesque. I'm being grotesque. That's good. Do you know how grotesque you're being? Nauseatingly grotesque.'

'Jack. . . .' She put out a hand and touched his shoulder. He shuddered her hand away.

'Don't you touch me.'

Roger took Helen's hand in his.

'You'll have to get over your nausea, young man, because your mother and I love each other and. . . .'

'Love . . . what do you mean love?'

'I'm sorry that you don't know the meaning of the word yourself.'

'She didn't love my father. How can she love someone like you? You're both making fools of yourselves.'

Helen uncoupled her hand from Roger's.

'You go home, darling. Jack will pull himself together and then we'll talk about all this. Just Jack and I will talk about it.' She smiled at him and nodded her head.

'Are you sure?'

'Quite sure.'

She put her arms around his neck and kissed his mouth.

'I love you.'

He held her for a moment.

'Yes,' he said.

As he moved across the room, Jack suddenly became aware of what was happening.

'No. Don't go.' He made a move to follow Roger, but Helen took hold of his arm.

'I'm sorry,' he said. He pulled at her fingers. 'I'm sorry. Stay. Let's talk.' Roger, in the doorway, raised his hand and smiled at Helen.

'Courage,' was all he said.

'Roger,' called out Jack.

Helen took hold of his shoulders and pushed him down into a chair.

'Call him back, Mother. I'm sorry. I was stupid. Please. . . .'

'Don't be silly, Jack. If you want to have a vile conversation, have it with me. I don't want him hurt.'

Jack gave her a push that sent her sprawling onto the floor. He jumped out of the chair and was away out of the room.

'Roger.'

She heard his voice in the hall.

'Roger.'

She heard him almost wail outside in the road.

Roger's car drove off and then after a moment Jack followed. For some inexplicable reason he had his hand on the horn and she heard the blaring twist away along the road.

She got up from the floor.

How absurd we are, she thought. How easily we become affected by panic. I will be calm, domestic. I will clear away the signs of our panic. I will open the wine, bang the cushions, set straight the rugs, polish the glasses. They will be back soon and there will be no more panic.

Then there was the first explosion. The house shivered and the glass in the window cracked from the top down to the bottom, and shards, slivers, splinters, slid scattered across the floor.

I didn't think that anything else mattered.

As in a fugue the shattering glass recurs and recurs, punctuates the rhythm of my life. New endings, new beginnings occur. Each shattering unveils the eye. Damian pointed out to me, though, that there was one fact about which only he and I were aware.

Neither the police, nor the coroner, judges, lawyers, nor the news men, nor the casual devourers of news, no one at all in fact was aware of the presence of Manus at the station on the night of the explosion. There was no trace, no inkling of his presence, though we knew that he must have been there. He must have started running when he heard the blaring of Jack's horn. Up behind the station, onto the hill he must have run, off the roads and up among the whins and the grazing sheep.

After they had gathered together the bits and pieces, the sad human detritus from the hedges and the surrounding fields, after identifications, investigations, and enquiries, it was officially stated that four men had died. Two, young men, whose names I have forgotten, who had been in the lorry when the accident happened; poor Roger, half-drunk with wine and love; and Jack whose hand was still on the horn as he ran into the back of Roger's car.

Needless was Roger's word.

I mourn the needless dead.

The recollections that I keep in my head are part of my private being.

On canvas, I belong to the world. I record for those who wish to look, the pain and joy and loneliness and fear that I see with my inward and my outward eye.

All those questions.

God-given.

And no answers.

In moments of viciousness, I quite like to think of Manus running up over the bare hills. Cold hills with little shelter. I like to think of him alone, frightened, exposed under the bright moon, the flinty stars, running.

Running.

Running.